The lone bed in the room was occupied—by a beautiful blonde

Krista? Seth took a few steps forward, letting his eyes get used to the dark. The figure on the bed rolled over and moaned. One bare shoulder appeared, followed by a perky nipple.

Krista. What the hell was she doing in *his* cabin?

For a crazy instant Seth imagined her engineering the shared room to make her fantasy of sex with a stranger come true. Just as quickly he realized that was impossible.

So was he in *her* cabin by mistake? Did he have the wrong key? He certainly had the wrong bed!

This was nuts. Where could he go? He had no other key, it was midnight, the weather sucked and the office was deserted.

He was stuck.

This was completely…totally…entirely…

Hmm…interesting.

A red-blooded male and a hot-blooded female trapped in the middle of nowhere in the middle of a snowstorm in the middle of a dark cozy cabin.

Maybe Christmas had come early after all!

Dear Reader,

The inspiration for this book was the myth of Cupid and Psyche. Who can resist the idea of a woman who falls in love with a mysterious sexy stranger she meets only in the dark? Of course, Harlequin Blaze is the perfect place to detail that kind of introduction. Add in a WRONG BED scenario, and the heat is on.

I loved introducing shades of gray into my heroine Krista's black-and-white life, and having her sensual energy seduce the hero out of his loner existence. Add in the magic of Christmas in a great town like Boston, and the story took off.

Wishing everyone the joys of the holiday season!

Isabel Sharpe

P.S. Stop by and visit my Web site at www.IsabelSharpe.com.

Books by Isabel Sharpe

HARLEQUIN BLAZE

11—THE WILD SIDE
76—A TASTE OF FANTASY
126—TAKE ME TWICE
162—BEFORE I MELT AWAY
186—THRILL ME

"Love Is a Beach" ALWAYS A BRIDESMAID anthology

ALL I WANT...
Isabel Sharpe

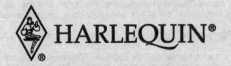

TORONTO • NEW YORK • LONDON
AMSTERDAM • PARIS • SYDNEY • HAMBURG
STOCKHOLM • ATHENS • TOKYO • MILAN • MADRID
PRAGUE • WARSAW • BUDAPEST • AUCKLAND

To Nancy Warren,
who has listened endlessly, advised wisely,
smacked me when I needed it
and been an unfailing, true friend

ISBN 0-373-79225-5

ALL I WANT…

Copyright © 2005 by Muna Shehadi Sill.

www.eHarlequin.com

Printed in U.S.A.

1

THE MINUTE AIMEE Wellington enters stage right in the new musical *Sweatshock,* all interest exits. Oh wait, no, hang on, not all interest! There's the can't-look/must-look fascinated horror of watching a speeding train heading for a stalled busload of nuns and orphans.

Has this woman or anyone handling her ever heard of the following concepts: Voice lessons? Acting lessons? Clue lessons? Pinocchio was less wooden. Adelaide from *Guys and Dolls* less nasal. The Invisible Man had more stage presence.

Could they not find one actress in Boston who could carry a tune, read lines with something approaching natural delivery or look like she was part of the ensemble instead of a wiggly, sexual me-me-me prop?

Oh, right, sorry, what was I thinking? It's not about talent. With Aimee Wellington it's never about talent. It's about money. It's about a chain of department stores that made her family fortune. It's about a father's decision to let her at that fortune way before she was mature enough to handle it. It's about getting famous by being infamous.

What happened to getting the best cast possible? Is the public that celebrity-crazed?

A sad state of affairs. From my seat, watching Aimee's two-expression acting and listening to her off-key whiny singing, I was very tempted to haul out a miniature dart gun and shoot her with a tranquilizer. Surely whomever they have understudying her would be less painful. Heck, put *me* on the stage!

And get real!

KRISTA MARLOW READ through her latest blog post again, crunching thoughtfully on natural-sea-salt potato chips she shouldn't be crunching on, thoughtfully or not, if she wanted to keep her weight at a healthy level. She'd started by bringing a sensible serving size out in a little red plastic bowl, one of the ones she and her sister used to have backyard picnic lunches in as kids, which she wouldn't let her mom throw away. But after three sensible serving sizes, she got tired of getting up and down—and even more tired of being sensible—so she brought the whole bag in and balanced it on the stack of papers and novels teetering on her desk.

Sometimes potato chips were necessary. This was one of those times.

Aimee Wellington drove Krista crazy. Not only because Krista's sister, Lucy, who could sing, act and dance circles around Aimee, had also been up for the part of Bridget in *Sweatshock* after Krista had practically dragged her to the audition. But just on principle. There were too many image-created idiots ruling showbiz—voices electronically enhanced and pitch-corrected, bodies surgically altered to some artificial ideal of perfection. And don't get her started on teenagers selling sex before they should be having it themselves.

Okay, so she sounded like someone's grandmother. And yes, she'd lost her virginity in her teens. But she wasn't out there pushing the experience on everyone else's kids. It hurt to see talent such as her sister's being wasted. To see her working a brainless office job, performing lounge gigs at night only a handful of white-hairs went to see, while no-talent prima-donna princesses rose to the top, like scum in a stockpot.

Krista's personal pilgrimage was to chip away at glossy facades, to point out in her blogs, Internet articles and pieces for the *Boston Sentinel* or any print media she could sell to, how people were being fooled by so much crap, into thinking crap was good. Her editor kept hinting that a staff reviewer was retiring soon, but Krista wanted to be like an octopus, tentacles spreading her message in all directions.

Call her crazy, call her a visionary, call her obsessed, but she wanted to leave her mark. Start some movement back to quality and a more natural rhythm to people's money-and-time-obsessed existences.

She'd started her own blogging Web site, Get Real, where she regularly skewered whatever artifice came to her attention. This new overpackaged, overprocessed gimmicky food product, that new undeserving star, this new over-the-top vacation destination which resembled a theme park more than a hotel. The Christmas holiday season had sparked a whole new crop of outrage over rampant commercialism, pressure to spend and compete, consumption-crazed children and *ho ho ho, goodwill to all*

*men, now get the hell out of my way before I ram you with
my shopping cart.*

Jeff Sites, a regular columnist at the *Boston Sentinel*,
had mentioned her rants in one of his Local Life columns
and her Web site hits had gone off the chart.

Happiness.

The more people who stopped and thought about what
crap they were supporting with their hard-earned dollars,
the more she hoped they'd vote with their wallets and de-
mand quality. Or keep their wallets in their pockets, stay
home and sing songs with their kids or play with the over-
load of stuff they already had. Leave the merchants and
marketers scrambling for something else with real appeal.

Like good quality at affordable prices.

She posted the blog and peered, yawning, at the clock
in the bottom right corner of her computer screen. *Oops.*
Nearly midnight. She needed her beauty rest.

One glance around her one-bedroom walk-up and
Krista sighed. And she needed cleaner surroundings.

She stood, stretching her shoulder and back muscles—
always tight no matter how many relaxation techniques
she tried—grabbed the bag of chips, folded the top and
headed for her kitchen and the pile of dirty dishes in the
sink. She always did them before bed. A new day required
a clean, organized living space.

Okay, mostly organized. Primarily clean. Hygienic
certainly.

Dishes done and a bottle of water grabbed from her
squeaky refrigerator—which needed cleaning, sigh—she
brushed her teeth and went into her bedroom, carpeted
with the same icky brown-orange shag as the kitchen/liv-
ing/dining room. Someday she'd own a fabulous place,

maybe in Cambridge, maybe down by the harbor, with hardwood floors and woven wool rugs. When her popularity and message caught on. When she wrote her first book. When she got her first appearance on Oprah…

Oops. Live in the moment. She forgot.

She began her nightly routine by standing in mountain pose, tall and still in the fairly small space between her bed and the wall, and concentrated on clearing her mind, concentrated on the sensations in her body and the play of her muscles holding her up. Spine straight, chin parallel to the floor…

Next, she started the sun salute, breathe in, out, arms in prayer position; breathe in, reaching up, palms facing; breathe out, swan dive to a forward fold, bent at the waist, trying to get her face to touch her knees.

As if.

Breathe in, right leg back in a runner's lunge….

Maybe she should do an article for a women's magazine on the benefits of a daily yoga routine, couching it in humor, focusing on spiritual satisfaction as a way to reduce spending for things one didn't need, not being preachy, just—

Mind clear, Krista.

Breathe in, breathe out. Her body followed the positions automatically. Breathe in, breathe out….

Tomorrow she would research the article she was proposing to *Budget Travel* magazine, about off-the-beaten-track, affordable holiday getaways. Romantic escapes from the pressures of the season. She could jot down a few ideas for the yoga article, too. And she needed to get going on one for *Food & Wine* about the country's love affair with oversalting and artificial flavor. She was thinking about calling it "Chemical Attraction."

Mind clear, Krista. Damn. She could never quite manage it.

Her phone rang and she gave up attempting inner peace and grabbed it. Only Lucy would call at this hour, home from her Tuesday night gig singing at Eddie's.

"Hey, Krista."

Krista frowned. Her younger sister didn't exactly sound jubilant. But then, she'd been sort of a pale imitation of herself for a while. "Bad show tonight?"

"Not terrific. Usually it's such a nice crowd. Tonight this drunk guy kept propositioning me during *When I Fall In Love,* and a few too many people acted as if I was a videotape in their living rooms and they were free to shout to each other whenever the mood hit." She sounded close to tears.

Bingo. An article or blog about technology-saturated people's newfound unfamiliarity with live entertainment and audience etiquette. Krista kept the phone to her ear and dragged off her sweats, letting the silence lag so her sister would fill it. Something else was really bothering Lucy. She knew the pitfalls of her business and had dealt with crowds much rougher than this one sounded.

"Then I got home and Link and I...we're barely speaking."

Krista cringed. Lincoln Baxter had been Lucy's unofficial fiancé for four years. Krista was sorry, and maybe she was being overly judgmental, but if you really wanted to marry someone, why didn't you do it? They'd been together six years, since their senior year at Tufts, and in Krista's opinion, the shine was off and they'd do better finding someone new. Link hadn't even managed to come up with a ring yet.

"He spends every evening watching TV. I just wish he'd spend some of that time with me. He never comes to hear me sing anymore, not that I blame him, but it would be nice, and I've asked him to. He stays up until all hours, we almost never go to bed at the same time, and when we do…well, nothing happens."

Krista winced and tossed her sweats on the chair next to her bed. She was getting the message. No sex, no intimacy. Might as well buy a male blow-up doll.

Hmm, maybe an article about artificial behaviors in men during courtship. Or make that artificial behaviors in women, too, so she wouldn't go on record as a man hater. Since she was, in fact, definitely not one, though with the mostly off-again unsatisfying state of her love life she was starting to consider it.

"Lucy, I think it's time to take a look at this relationship."

"No, no." The fear in Lucy's voice made Krista's heart sink. "It's not that bad."

"You can't stay with him because you're afraid of being alone."

"He's the man for me, Krista. I've known since the second I set eyes on him."

Right. Krista fumbled for her pink flannel nightgown under her bed pillows. She believed in that love-at-first-sight stuff exactly not at all. Chemistry she believed in, instant attraction she believed in, but love took time. Love was what was left when infatuation finally got bored and took a hike. Love was what she saw in her parents' eyes every time they looked at each other.

Okay, not every time. When Dad put off cleaning the garage too long or mom took three days to make a simple decision…

"Neither of you is the same person as in college." She lifted her arms one at a time to slip the nightgown over her head, whipping the phone around the neckline and back to her ear. "People change. You grew apart."

"We're just in a rut right now. We need something. I don't know what."

"Counseling?"

"He won't go."

"Lucy, you really—"

"I gotta go, he's coming to bed. Lunch Thursday?"

"Sure." Krista hung up the phone and scrunched her face in a scowl. Her sister was incredibly sweet and incredibly talented and deserved to be riding the wave of love and stardom all the way to happy ever after. Instead she'd been upstaged by a bimbo and had shackled herself to a man indifferent to what made her so special. Loyalty, talent, intelligence, empathy, sex appeal, beauty, sparkle— well, she used to sparkle. Now she just glowed dully through mucky layers of disappointment.

Krista put in her earplugs and slid into bed. If Lucy had gotten the part in *Sweatshock,* she'd be in a position of power, and Krista would bet a million she'd have the strength to leave Link and find someone who deserved her. A new love that fit the dynamic, fabulous person she was now.

Just another grudge to hold against the inimitable— thank God—Aimee Wellington.

SETH WELLINGTON SAT sprawled in his favorite black leather chair, set near the giant living room window of his South Boston condo, whose view of the harbor reminded him daily there was more to the world than gray four-walled corporate boardrooms. A timely thought. He grimaced at the computer screen on his laptop, which showed the blog fellow board member Mary Stevens had sent him the link to. This Krista Marlow woman had a serious grudge against his stepsister, Aimee. He'd seen *Sweatshock* the previous week, and while Aimee would never be Renée Zellweger, neither was she as bad as this sarcastic, clearly unhappy person made her out to be.

Bad timing. As the interim CEO of Wellington Department Stores while his father recovered from a stroke, he'd spent his tenure trying to convince the board of directors to update the stores' stodgy image. The trouble with inheriting a dinosaur—er, *dynasty*—that stretched back into the late nineteenth century was that, like the dinosaurs who went extinct rather than adapt, some members of the board seemed to want everything to stay the same as when Seth's ancestor Oscar Wellington opened the first store near Copley Square in 1889.

Seth and Mary were the newest and, at thirty-six and thirty-nine respectively, by far the youngest board members. Over the last year-plus they'd fought long and hard for the changes, territory won, territory lost, two steps forward, one back. Finally their efforts would pay off, God willing, with the official reopening of the stores, December twenty-first. Of course he would rather have launched the new image *before* the most profitable time of the year, but the board had been a bigger problem than he'd anticipated and the contractors hadn't shared his sense of urgency.

Aimee had been Seth's choice for the stores' new spokesperson. She'd done a great job in the hip, upbeat musical commercials that would begin airing in sync with the reopening. Given that Aimee was Aimee, her duties representing the stores publicly could be a dicier prospect. But she was family, the all-important connection so vital to Seth's dad; she sported the Wellington name via Seth's father's remarriage. And her performing experience made her a natural in front of the cameras, where she'd get most of her exposure—literally, given her skimpy outfits. Aimee could bridge the gap between older loyal customers and new ones the stores hadn't been attracting in large enough numbers no matter how up-to-date they kept their merchandise.

But Krista Marlow was making Aimee look more like a joke than Aimee did herself. The board members were not amused. They felt Krista's potential for damage was minimal when her war had been waged locally, focusing on Aimee's notorious shopping exploits and her enthusiastic if misguided obsession with performing and self-promotion. But with media attention surrounding the reopening and with commercials scheduled to air throughout New England, the board feared Krista's biased opinions would reach a much wider audience and make a mockery of the new image they'd been against from the beginning.

Could Krista really do the stores any damage? In his view, most likely not. Ironically her rants might even help. No publicity was bad publicity, as the cliché went. But he had to admit, Krista's vitriol rankled. Had to admit he took it personally, not only being Aimee's stepbrother but also having invested so much of his life into the Wellington stores. Given that he hadn't exactly volunteered for this CEO job, he'd be damned if his sweat and sacrifice led to failure of any kind.

His cell rang. He put the laptop aside, dug the phone out warily from his pocket, then relaxed and smiled at the number on the display. Mary. He'd been dodging board member calls for the last hour, not in the mood for more concerns now that they'd undoubtedly read Marlow's latest attack on his stepsister. Tedious bunch. *Ms. Marlow must be stopped before she ruins the Wellington name*, blah, blah, blah.

Any wonder he'd rather be out experiencing the real world as he was meant to? After he'd graduated from business school, what was supposed to be a month-long traveling vacation had turned into two months, then six, then over a year, until his father's poor health brought Seth back to the company he'd worked for since he was old enough to alphabetize.

Family was family, yes. Though at times family life felt more like being incarcerated at Alcatraz.

"Hi, Mary."

"Did you get the link I sent you? I've gotten three calls already from board members squawking something fierce."

"I got it." He kept his voice from sounding too weary. "Looks like Ms. Marlow didn't enjoy the show."

"Ya think? If I hear 'This could have serious consequences' one more time, I'm going to book a ticket to Jamaica and drink rum until it's all over. Want to come?"

He grinned. His affair with Mary had burned hot and briefly; instant attraction had been indulged, waned, and they'd settled into a fairly comfortable friendship. Occasionally they still got together, but they'd been successful keeping their personal lives off the company gossip sheet. She was the kind of woman he liked. Smart, sexy, discreet and, best of all, not clingy. She never took their relationship to be anything but what it was.

"Sounds like paradise right about now. How often have we reassured them the risk is minimal?"

"Too many times."

He grabbed the back of his neck and tried to massage a dent in the knotted muscles, gazing out at the black expanse of ocean with longing. Jumping for people was the part of this job he hated most. "As much as I don't want to get involved, with everything else we have to do, maybe it wouldn't hurt to be seen taking steps, so these fine gentlemen can put a sock in it."

And maybe they had the smallest point. He'd just as soon people didn't keep tabs on the stores only to see if Aimee made an idiot of herself, which, given Aimee, was always a distinct possibility, though he'd decided she was worth the risk. But if people came to associate the stores with someone they didn't respect, Seth would have to concede the Wellington image could suffer—and the board's opinion of him would certainly tank. Yes, he wanted out of the CEO job, but he wanted out because his father was well enough to take over the company again, not because he'd run it into the ground.

"So you're going to take her on?"

He sighed. "I'll think of something. The bare minimum that will satisfy the board."

"Ooooh." Mary laughed, deep and sexy. "Should I scan the headlines tomorrow for news of Ms. Marlow dredged out of the Charles River wearing designer cement shoes?"

"I don't think it will come to that."

"Mmm, I hope not. I'd hate to lose you to jail time."

He chuckled. "No chance of that. Thanks for letting me know about the blog, Mary."

"You're welcome. Call anytime you want to talk." She used the husky tone that said "talk" wasn't on her mind.

"I will. Good night." He hung up, aware she'd been about to say more, feeling a twinge of guilt. But if he gave her an inch now, she'd grab for...seven. And he wasn't in the mood for that kind of fun. Every ounce of his energy and concentration was necessary to make sure the revamping of the stores wasn't going to be a colossal, extremely expensive and humiliating failure.

He swallowed the last tepid sip of after-dinner coffee and stood, bringing his favorite mug—one his mom bought him when he took her to Graceland, before she'd gotten too sick to travel—into his kitchen. He washed and dried it carefully and put it next to the coffeemaker, already sporting a new filter for the next morning's brew. A quick wipe-down of the counters, and he filled a big glass with filtered water from his stainless refrigerator's door dispenser.

After that, a check of the downstairs rooms to make sure they were tidy and locked up tight, then he went upstairs to his second-floor loft in the condo he'd bought even though he wouldn't be staying long.

He strode into his bedroom, undressed and retrieved the top paperback from a neat stack under his night table. The latest Harlan Coben thriller. He needed some distraction, somewhere to go that was under control, precise, unpolluted by the wandering vagaries of real human existence.

Ten minutes later he gave up the pretense at reading. Even page-turning excitement couldn't distract him from his growing irritation.

He turned off his light and drew up the blankets. Lay, hands folded behind his head, staring at the dotted stripes of light on his ceiling from the punched holes and chinks in his blinds. He didn't have time for worrying about one woman's opinion.

And yet something about Krista Marlow's disrespect toward Aimee bordered on illogical. Something about it was too...personal. Yeah, she was funny as hell, spirited and right-on in a lot of what she said. After her first post about Aimee, he'd started checking in occasionally and had been interested by most of what she had to say.

Then a couple of months ago, after Aimee's joke of a self-produced CD came out, around the time she landed the part in *Sweatshock,* the attacks on Aimee became more frequent and more cutting.

He frowned and shifted between the sheets. Admittedly he was curious.

Tomorrow he'd try to find out more about Marlow, something reassuring to report to the board. Maybe tell them he'd ask her to ease up. Worth a try. With Wellington Stores' grand reopening on the horizon, he needed the board one hundred percent behind him. Even a small glitch was more of a glitch than he wanted.

Because the sooner he could turn the company around, the sooner he could hand the running of it back to his father, and leave again.

LUCY MARLOW SLIPPED out of the bed she shared with Link in their beautiful Cambridge condo and tiptoed out of the room. Three in the morning and she hadn't even managed to close her eyes. Insomnia wasn't new to her, but lately she'd been bursting into tears for no apparent reason, and she couldn't stay in bed and cry. Link would waken, he'd want to know what was wrong. And how often could she say "nothing" or "I don't know" without him rolling his eyes as men had been rolling their eyes at those answers for centuries, maybe millennia?

She went into their living room, chilly with the heat turned down at night, and curled up on the window seat, looking out at the parked cars on Garden Street. This time of year was always tough, when the calendar said ho ho ho, merry merry, happy happy, and somehow her mood and stress levels never quite made it there. Gifts to buy for Link, for Mom and Dad, for Krista, for Link's relatives, her relatives, friends, coworkers. She made it harder on herself, she knew that, and Link was always telling her as if he thought she didn't. Having to find the perfect presents, having to decorate the house, having to make cookies and volunteer and organize the office party…

An old Volkswagen van putted by, like the relic her parents had when she was very young. That seemed to be enough to trigger the insane tears that were her all-too-regular visitors these days.

Was this simple unhappiness? She didn't feel unhappy, necessarily. She had a lovely home in a beautiful city. She was engaged to a man she loved, though he didn't seem to be in any hurry to get married or buy her a ring.

They weren't ready for children, Link said, and what difference did a piece of paper make in how they felt about each other?

Logically? Intellectually? No difference.

But emotionally…

Well, women were the emotional ones, weren't they. He'd marry her if she insisted, she knew that. But she couldn't bring herself to insist. She didn't ever want to be standing up at an altar without being one hundred percent

sure the man next to her would rather be there than anywhere else in the world. Marriage should be entered into
gladly and with light hearts.

These days her heart was about as light as a brick.

The beautiful, sad tears turned to fairly unattractive
sobs she fought hard to keep as silent as possible. Link
slept like a rock, but you never knew.

Everything else about her life was going fine. She had a
nice job as an administrative assistant in a law firm downtown. She'd chosen the work deliberately, to keep her mind
and energies fresh for performing, though these days she'd
made friends with her limitations there. Lucy's natural re-
serve was her enemy on stage—people like Aimee would always get ahead. While Krista would cheerfully disembowel
the poor woman, Lucy understood the casting decision.

In retrospect, she'd taken the audition more to please
Krista than herself anyway. Krista had enough ambition
to spare for everyone. Lucy was a creature of habit, of routine. Unlike her sister, she wasn't comfortable or happy
constantly searching for new heights to scale.

What was really important to her? Family, friends and
Link. Not in that order of course. She had a close family,
a lot of friends locally. The people in the law firm were
wonderful and kind. Her boss, Alexis, was fair and pleasant. One of the lawyers, Josh, had even been flirting with
her lately, and that was harmless fun.

A thrill ran through her and she curled the fingers of
her left hand, feeling the missing ring keenly tonight. Josh
knew about Link, he knew about their so-called engage-
ment, but he kept coming around, and lately she hadn't
done enough to discourage him. A ring would make her
feel more taken, show the world she belonged to Link in

a way she wasn't sure the world knew right now. And maybe not her either.

Because she *was* taken. Thoroughly. Just because Josh turned her insides over and around and upside down when he smiled at her...

She spun suddenly to face the room. So? Plenty of happily married—or involved—people developed crushes which had no significance and faded. She'd had them, too, once or twice in the years she and Link had been together.

The intensity of this one stemmed from it hitting when she was particularly vulnerable. When she and Link were having a particularly bad time. When she was not at all sure why or how to go about fixing whatever had gone wrong. Relationships inevitably encountered rough patches, but this one seemed...ominous. Lately she'd been wondering how much longer she could go on without listening to the doubting voices in her head, without looking at the discouraging signs along the way.

Tonight she'd come home from singing at Eddie's to find the dinner dishes still stacked in the sink, Link sprawled in front of the TV. She'd gone to him, kissed him, he'd mumbled a question about how the show had gone, and had barely noticed her response. Then she'd gone into the kitchen, cleaned up, made her lunch for the next day, hearing the canned laugh track mingle with Link's occasional laughter, louder than his usual. It was hard not to feel as though he was rubbing it in that he was enjoying himself while she slaved.

But she couldn't think that way. Link worked hard, too—most architects did, long hours and often late—and she wanted him to have his wind-down time, his leisure.

She just wanted him to need her with him enough so that maybe one day he'd turn off the TV and come in and help her. Really talk to her and really listen. The way he used to.

But those things she had no control over. She wanted him, but she couldn't make him want her.

Lucy sighed and pulled her feet up on the window seat, arms around her knees. Big sister Krista would tell her to get therapy or go on antidepressants or kick herself out of it.

Krista would tell her to leave Link and start a relationship with Josh.

Krista had never been in love. Though what Lucy called love, Krista called codependency—or had once in a particularly bitter argument in the ongoing series of arguments they'd been having about Lucy's relationship.

Everything in Krista's life was crystal clear, black or white, right or wrong. She knew unswervingly how everyone around her was supposed to behave in every situation she and everyone else found themselves in.

Sometimes Lucy thought nothing would make her happier than for Krista to fall passionately, inextricably in love in a situation so complicated and hopeless that her world would turn upside down and she'd be reduced to angsting uncertainly over every aspect of her existence for hours at a time.

But then, that wasn't particularly sisterly or charitable of her, was it.

Mom would say she was going through a stage, that love was hard and life had its yin and yang and she needed to buckle down and chin up and get through it.

Dad would chuck her under the chin and wish fervently that his little girl would be happy, then go back to watching the Celtics.

Link would look at her like why was she making such a big deal out of everything? With the implied "again" at the end. Life is beautiful, he'd say. You wake up, you do stuff you enjoy, you go to bed.

Wake up. Do stuff. Go to bed. Every day. Yes, but there used to be more magic, even in that.

The tears slowed; she sniffed and wiped them away with the back of her hand.

A slight sound made her jump; she turned to see Link, bed-ruffled, puzzled, half-asleep, swaying in the doorway, his tall, beautifully muscled body illuminated by the white light from the street behind her.

"Lucy." He frowned and peered at her across the room. "Why'd you get out of bed?"

"I couldn't sleep."

He squinted and took a step toward her. "Are you crying?"

She hesitated. If she said no, she'd be lying. If she said yes, she'd have to explain.

"Sort of."

"What do you mean sort of?" The irritation was starting in his voice already. It seemed to be his regular tone of communication these days. "Are you crying or not?"

"I was."

"Why?"

"Go back to bed, Link. I'll be fine."

"Why are you crying?"

"It's nothing."

He made a sound of exasperation. "You're sitting here crying in the middle of the night in the dark for no reason."

"Yes." She barely got the word out for the hot, miserable weight in her chest.

He put his hands on his hips, glaring at her. Opened his

mouth to say something, then lifted one hand and let it slap on his flannel-covered thigh. "Fine. No reason. Good night."

He walked out of the room, stumbled and swore. She heard the headboard bounce against the wall as he flung himself into their bed. He'd sleep badly now and blame it on her. Wake up in a bad mood and they'd eat the breakfast she prepared in a silence that was starting to become horribly familiar.

Lucy hugged her knees close to her chest, rested her chin on top of them and let the tears flow again.

She loved Link. Loved him with all her heart and had since they'd first met in college—six years ago at the beginning of their senior year—and begun dating within a week.

But something wasn't working. She didn't know what it was or when it had happened or even how to identify it so she could begin to fix it.

And she was terribly, deathly afraid it would end up tearing them apart.

2

SETH SWAGGERED INTO the offices of the *Boston Sentinel*, sunglasses on, Red Sox cap pulled firmly onto his head. A tiny gold hoop hung off his left ear, and his knees had felt the December breeze through the holes in his jeans. The hood of his sweatshirt bounced against his upper back as he walked. He had a major 'tude going. And he who had expected to be seething with resentment over this utter waste of his time…was having a ball.

Not a soul would recognize him as Seth Wellington IV, heir to the vast Wellington fortune, CEO of the very respectable company. He hadn't done anything like this in almost two years. Not since his traveling days, when he'd experimented with different personalities in different towns, tried them on to see how people reacted.

Er, okay, mostly to see how women reacted.

He approached the receptionist, a young perky blonde, and leaned his forearms on her desk, wishing he could whip off his sunglasses and make eye contact but not daring to reveal that much of his face. "Hey, how you doing today?"

"I'm fine, thank you." She held herself formally, but a tiny smile was trying to curve her lips. "Can I help you?"

"Sure, yeah. I'm Bobby Darwin, old classmate of Krista. Is she here?"

"Krista..."

"Yeah." He grinned at her. "Marlow."

"She was in this morning. You just missed her."

"Damn." He slapped the desk and straightened, hands on his hips, shaking his head. "Missed her at home, now here. You know where she went?"

"She said she was going to lunch."

"Yeah?" He opened his eyes wide, looking appalled. "And she didn't invite you?"

The receptionist giggled, blushing peaches and cream. "No."

He leaned forward again. What he wouldn't give to be twenty-two again and free to charm this one into a date. "What's your name?"

"Charlisse."

"Well, let me ask you this, Charlisse. You know where she was heading? I'd kinda like to surprise her, you know? We've known each other, whoa—" he shook his head as if he couldn't believe how many years had gone by "—long time. I'm in town, thought I'd look her up and surprise her, but I keep just missing her. What's up with that?"

Charlisse giggled, clearly warming to him. "I don't know. Bad karma maybe."

"Exactly." He let the silence go a beat too long. "So Charlisse, can you do something for me?"

"What?" She tilted her head and looked at him coyly.

"Well..." He turned right and left, as if checking for eavesdroppers, then leaned on her desk again. "Can you turn that bad karma around and tell me where she went?"

"Um..." Charlisse frowned and her pink, edible mouth twisted.

"I'm not a creep. I swear." He stood up and crossed himself. "I'm a good Catholic boy, schooled by nuns."

Charlisse giggled, reminding him of Aimee. "Well, if I was going to tell you, I think I'd tell you she has a lunch date with her sister at Thai Banquet around the corner from Symphony Hall."

"Fabulous. You are beautiful, Charlisse, thanks." He backed away a few steps, then stopped and spread out his hands. "If I had roses, I'd give you some."

"You're welcome." She giggled again and reached for the ringing phone.

He waved, strode back down the hall and stepped out into the chill, breath frosting, adrenaline pumping. That was serious fun. He'd found some information about Marlow this morning on the Internet, including that she'd gone to Framingham High School. He got the name Bobby Darwin from one of those online find-your-classmate sites. Who knew what Bobby Darwin looked like now or where he was or whether she knew him in high school. It didn't matter. Even if she was still best friends with him and figured out Seth was an imposter when Charlisse mentioned him, he'd be long gone, back into his Prada and paperwork, back inhabiting his father's office.

Around the corner from the *Sentinel,* Frank, his driver, pulled the car up to the curb. Seth wasn't wild about the idea of a chauffeur, even less about being driven in a 1988 Lincoln Town Car, but Frank had been in his father's employ for twenty years and would be able to retire in three. Seth didn't have the heart to fire him. Frank loved the car, and with the traffic in downtown Boston, a vehicle Seth didn't have to find a parking space for was a godsend.

From the backseat he directed Frank to Thai Banquet,

took off the hat, sweatshirt and earring and changed into wool suit pants, perfectly polished shoes and his lightly starched white shirt, feeling his giddy excitement shutting down further with each button. A respectable businessman once again. Damned depressing.

The car pulled up opposite the Thai restaurant, known for inventive curries and fabulous noodle dishes. One thing he could say about Krista, she knew her Thai food. The place was one of his favorites.

He thanked Frank and emerged into the street, stepped up on the sidewalk and strode to the restaurant front door, decorated with green and red blinking lights for the season. What new information could he discover about Ms. Marlow beyond the basic résumé stuff? Ohio Wesleyan University as a journalism major. Links to articles she'd written. But nothing that explained why she was targeting his stepsister.

If she was eating with her sister, chances were he'd hit the jackpot. Women close to each other couldn't help spilling every bit of their souls at every meeting. Exhausting to his way of thinking. His local friendships were pretty basic "guy" friendships, not that he'd been in touch with many of them since he'd been back in town. *How 'bout them Red Sox?* and *How's the golf game?* and *Angelina Jolie...whoa.* He liked them that way. His soul belonged to himself—he saw no reason to empty it onto other people at regular intervals.

Inside the restaurant, inhaling the blissful scents of curry and galangal and lemongrass, he discovered another stroke of luck—Ms. Marlow was eating late and the regular lunch crowd had thinned, leaving him a better shot at sitting close by. He kept on his sunglasses and smiled at Panjai, the hostess, while scanning the diners. Now if Krista would just do him the favor of looking exactly like the fairly plain, gawky high school photo he'd found online....

Uh...no.

Blond and blue-eyed hadn't changed, but plain and gawky had fled. She now sported one of those wispy, flippy hairstyles that made her look elfin and very, very appealing.

Krista Marlow was not what he'd expected. She was sexy as hell.

She laughed at something her sister said and her face came even more alive with energy and radiance.

Wow.

She was tiny, slender, and dressed fashionably in a black-and-white sweater with pink accents. He'd expected a butch Amazon with a dour expression, dragging on a cigarette and pontificating in a growly voice about how no one deserved to live but her and those select few who could make her life easier.

He requested the booth next to the sisters, keeping his face averted as he passed. From his seat directly behind Krista he'd be able to eavesdrop shamelessly. A peek before he sat told him they'd just been served their entreés, so he'd have some time to listen, though he needed to be back in his office by three for a conference call with the new head buyer he'd hired. Which sounded a lot less fun than what he was doing right now.

Because it was.

Marasri came by to take his order, a round, matronly woman he particularly liked who got her job done with remarkable efficiency for someone who seemed never to move quickly. She filled his water glass and winked. "You ready? You don't need to look at the menu, I know."

"I'll have the chef special soup and green curry chicken, please."

"No Singha?"

He grinned and shook his head. "No beer today. I have to get back to work."

"Ah, you work too hard." She shook her head disapprovingly. "You need to play more."

He shrugged. If she only knew. "Who has time?"

Marasri gave him a you'll-never-learn look and ambled off to put in his order. Seth leaned back, ready to listen to whatever his stepsister's thorn chose to say. With any luck, the conversation would turn to Aimee, and he'd get some idea where the extra dose of bitterness and sarcasm Krista reserved for her came from.

But even if the conversation stayed on other topics, he had to admit he was just plain curious about her. After reading her blogs and some of her articles, this Krista Marlow person intrigued him.

Probably more than he wanted her to.

"So." LUCY FORKED UP a pineapple chunk from her yellow curry shrimp and tasted it gingerly. "What's next for you workwise?"

"Oh, let's see…" Krista glanced up as a thirty-something man in a business suit walked past and took a seat in the booth behind her. Unfortunately she didn't get much of a look, but he gave the impression of being attractive.

She turned her attention back to Lucy's question, digging into her pad thai noodles, wondering when she could safely change the subject to Link and the need, in her opinion, for him to be extracted from Lucy's life. "Travel, actually. I'm doing a story about affordable off-the-beaten-track romantic getaways for couples wanting to escape holiday pressures. Maybe you and Link…"

Lucy was already shaking her head. "He'd say it sounded remote and chilly."

Krista shrugged, thinking she could say the same about Link lately. "People shouldn't have to suffer through all this holiday stress. Christmas should be about love—family love, romantic love, religious love. Love and traditions, like our family's, caroling and candelabra lighting and making Christmas Eve dinner together. Anything but buy, buy, buy and then buy more and, while you're at it, buy again…"

She stopped when Lucy's eyes glazed over. Okay, so she preached her version of the gospel too often. "Anyway, I leave tomorrow for Maine. A place called Pine Tree Inn, way past Skowhegan."

"Which is…?"

"On the road to nowhere. That's the point. Get this— forty-five dollars a night."

"And all the moose you can eat?"

Krista laughed and fluttered her eyelashes. "It sounds sooo romantic, no?"

"Alone?"

"Yeah, there is that." She sighed. Unfortunately alone was more familiar to her than involved. "I've decided to think of it as research for my next fling."

"The word is re-la-tion-ship." Lucy enunciated as if she was teaching a two-year-old something new. "Can you say that?"

"Ree-lay-shin…something." She shrugged helplessly. "I got the 'lay' part."

Lucy rolled her eyes, barely suppressing a smile. "Ha. Ha."

Krista grinned. She enjoyed playing the role of the great sexual predator. They both knew better, and it made Lucy smile, which Krista desperately wanted her to do more often. "And so, Ms. Lucy, speaking of ree-lay-mum-ble-mumbles..."

"Oh no."

"Come on, you knew I was going to ask. What's up with Lincoln?"

Lucy's beautiful face shut down and Krista wanted to put down her fork, reach across the table and shake some sense into her could-have-been-a-model, should-be-a-star sister. Fact one: Lucy was miserable with Link. Fact two: Lucy was miserable with Link. And it's ...fact three! He's outta there! The relationship is retired!

"Things are bad. I don't know what to do."

"Get out?"

Her eyes grew defensive. "Krista..."

"Lucy..."

Lucy sighed and chewed a tiny bite of shrimp as if it was enough for a whole meal.

"I know, I know." Krista waved her sister off. "You hate me saying that. But it seems obvious to me that—"

"Of *course* it seems obvious to you." She gestured with her shrimp-impaled fork. "*Everything* seems obvious to you. The fact is, I love this man."

"And...?" Krista looked at her blankly. "To quote Tina Turner, what's love got to do with it? He makes you unhappy. You aren't enjoying your day job, your performing career is stalled, you look tired and defeated.... Hello? What's wrong with this picture?"

"You don't understand."

Krista leaned forward on her elbows. "Try me."

"He is The One."

"The one what? The one guy you've ever dated seriously?"

"The One. The love of my life."

Krista let out a growl of exasperation. "Lucy, the issue is not whether you love him or not. The issue is that you're not good for each other anymore."

"We are." She tightened her lips, looking exactly as stubborn and scared as she had at ten when Krista had talked her out of a ladder-climbing dare she'd accepted from a neighbor kid. "We've just lost our way right now."

"Can I be totally brutally honest here?"

Lucy's expression turned incredulous. "Like you're ever not?"

"Point taken." She lifted her hands in surrender. "You're clinging to the past, to this ideal of Link that no longer exists, to this dream of marrying him and having babies and—"

"It's not a dream." Lucy's voice broke. "I *am* going to marry him and I *am*—"

"When?"

"When he's—when we're ready." She folded her arms across her chest and sank against the back of the booth.

"Think you'll get a ring at Christmas this year?"

"I don't know."

"But you're hoping?"

Lucy gave a small sad shrug. "It's all I want."

"Jeez, Lucy." Krista stared miserably at her sister. Didn't she hear what she sounded like? Was the person being stifled by a crappy relationship always the last to know? Or at least to admit it? "I'm watching the *Titanic* head for the iceberg here. You marry this guy, your shot at a lifeboat is gone. You think a ceremony is going to fix your problems?"

"No." Lucy lifted her chin and met Krista's eye defiantly. "But what we have is forever."

"That's a line from some sappy movie on the Lifetime Channel." She forced herself to lower and gentle her voice. "This is reality we're dealing with here. Or trying to."

"You don't understand. You've never been in love."

"I—" She snapped her mouth shut. *Kaboom.* There it was. The horrible, tremendous truth. Lust, oh yes, infatuation, sure, sometimes pretty strong. But love? Nope. Emphatically not. When her relationships ended, she was over it in a week, sometimes two. And she wasn't quite sure why.

She took a deep breath. "Okay, you're right. I haven't been. Not for real."

"Because you always fall for creeps."

Another deep breath. "But, I—"

"Bad boys who excite you for about twenty minutes until they ejaculate and run."

"Lucy…"

"Am I wrong?"

Krista wrinkled her nose. "Exaggerating maybe. But how about we get back to you?"

"I'd rather stay on this subject."

"Of *my* miserable failings? No way. We're talking about you and how it's not happening with you guys anymore."

"Relationships are work." Lucy stared at Krista pointedly. "If you'd had one that lasted more than the first thrilling months, you'd know."

Ouch. Okay, fair enough. But none of that took away from the fact that Lucy was unhappy and Krista hated seeing her that way. Working on relationships was one thing. Staying when there was nothing left to stay for was another.

She reached across the table to touch her sister's hand. "Answer this. Deep down, don't you really think it's over?"

Lucy's shoulders hunched. She dropped her eyes. "Link is a good person. I love him."

"Avoiding the ques-tion." Krista sang the words, but gently.

"We're…definitely in a bad place."

"Yes or no, Luce?"

"Kris…." She took a deep breath and blew it out. "Okay. I don't know how we can get past what's happening."

"*Now* we're getting some—"

"But I know we can if I can just figure it out."

Krista resisted rolling her eyes. But okay, she'd pushed plenty hard enough. Her runaway mouth had done its thing again. Like an alcoholic or a depressed person, Lucy had to get to that place of wanting to change by herself. All Krista could do was nudge occasionally—hard enough to get Lucy thinking but not so hard Lucy panicked and cleaved unto Link like mortar unto brick. "Okay. I'm done meddling. I'm sorry. I just want you to be happy."

"I know. I will be when we work this out." Lucy lowered her tensed shoulders and shook her head, forcing a cheerful expression. "You, on the other hand, are hopeless."

"Me?" Krista blinked innocently.

"Because you can't look past a hot body."

"Mmm, no."

"Or a cocky attitude."

"Ooh, you got that so right."

"Or the huge initial adrenaline rush of lust."

"Hit me, baby, one more time."

Lucy laughed and Krista grinned in response, wishing the subject of Link could put that smile on her face.

"See? Hopeless!"

"But at least I'm still out there trying for what I really want. If it doesn't show up soon, I'm happy playing for a few more years."

"Happy? Was that not you grumbling and moaning into your noodles two months ago when Robby stopped calling?"

"Oh. Yes." Krista heaved a wistful sigh. "Robby the Wonder Dick."

"Mmph." Lucy slammed down her water glass and covered her mouth to swallow carefully. "*Krista.*"

"Yes?"

"Someone might hear you."

"Who's going to hear me? And even if they did I'm sure they'd be happy for me. Getting skillfully laid is a very good thing."

"*Shhh.*" Lucy glanced around, beet-red.

Krista took pity on her. "No one is listening. And you know I go into every relationship hoping I'll get it right this time. You're just too fun to tease."

"Like when you told me I was adopted because my skin smelled wrong?"

"Ha! What about when you told Mom I was planning to throw red socks into a white load of wash and I wasn't?"

"Who added Shep's kibble to my party snack mix for Home Ec?"

"Who squirted disappearing ink on my white prom dress the second my date rang the doorbell?"

"Truce!" Lucy held up her little finger, crooked. Krista did the same. They locked pinkies and grinned.

"I just want everything to work out for you." Krista disengaged her pinkie and squeezed Lucy's hand.

"I know." Lucy looked dejectedly down at her barely touched curry. "I'll think of something."

"Well, in the meantime, eat. You're losing weight—and you have none to lose." Krista picked up her fork and shoveled in some more pad thai. She, on the other hand, could still eat heartily while being carried off by a tornado.

Lucy glanced up at Krista, then back down at her plate. She pushed her food around again with intense concentration it didn't deserve. "Um…Krista?"

Krista put down her fork. *Uh-oh.* This was going to be something big. "Yeah, hon?"

"I need to tell you something."

"I'm listening."

"There's this guy at my office…." A blush bloomed on Lucy's cheek.

Krista's eyes shot wide. "Omigod! Tell me. What's happening? He's into you? You're into him?"

Lucy kept her eyes down, but her cheeks were rapidly leaving pink behind in favor of red. "I guess…yeah. I'm so confused. It's… I'm so confused."

"Well, so what's happening?" Krista tried to sound calm, but she wanted to give herself a huge high-five. Yes! A possible escape route from being trapped in Lincoln hell! "Has he asked you out?"

"Yes. I can't go, of course. But he…I mean, he sort of makes me—"

"Ooooh. He does?"

Lucy jerked her head up, frowning. "You don't even know what I'm going to say."

"Hot. Crazy. Ready to tear your clothes off at the

merest glance from his endless, fathomless, fire-starting eyes."

"Yeah." Lucy whispered the word and a big fat tear slipped out of her eye. "That."

Krista's heart melted. "Oh, honey, don't cry. This is not bad. This is…wonderful. I mean—wait. Sheesh, what am I saying? Complicated is what it is."

"I know. I know." Lucy pressed her napkin to the corner of her eye. "This morning he asked me if I wanted to have a drink with him after work."

"And?"

"I said no. Of course I said no."

"But…you wanted to say yes?"

A tearful nod.

"Oh, boy." Krista took a deep breath, torn between sympathy and excitement that this might be the shove Lucy needed to move on to greener pastures. From there maybe onto the stage or screen where she belonged, where she'd make "stars" like Aimee into more of a parody than they made themselves.

"You know, Lucy, this might be a sign. I know I'm not in a position to give expert advice on anyone's love life. But if a man affects you that strongly…and considering that your relationship with Link has stalled out… Well, when someone makes you that crazy, I think you need to go with it."

"But I barely know him."

"You gotta start somewhere." She searched her brain for more arguments. Something had to click with Lucy. "You must be curious about him, aren't you?"

Another nod.

"I'm not suggesting cheating, just a drink—to see how it feels."

"But, Kris, this attraction is based on nothing. Link is real, I know him inside out. Josh is hormones and fantasy."

"So what's wrong with fantasy? When else are you going to get the chance to indulge one? You're always so damn sensible." Krista leaned forward. "You want to know my deepest, darkest, craziest fantasy?"

A piece of silverware clattered from the booth behind her.

"What?"

"Seeing someone that makes me that hot…and just going for it. Right then. Not even saying anything." She watched her sister's face brighten and she cheered silently. "Not worrying about a single consequence. Totally animal. Totally wild."

"But that's so dangerous, I mean it's…nuts." She breathed out a laugh, as if the idea was ludicrous, which of course it was…but exciting.

"Of course it's nuts. That's why it's only a fantasy. But Luce, you can have that fantasy with this guy, only in a safer context because you already know he's not a psycho." She put as much earnestness into her eyes as she could, willing Lucy to drop the safe habit and fling herself out there. This was Lucy's chance to escape.

"I couldn't do that to Link."

Krista clenched her teeth. "Have a drink with Josh, that's all I'm suggesting. If something is meant to be between you, the attraction will only get stronger. If not, you'll be able to get out with no guilt and no hard feelings."

Lucy shook her head. "I couldn't go behind Link's back."

"Then tell him." Krista kept her frustration hidden. "You're going to have a drink with a coworker, that's not immoral. Link doesn't own you."

Lucy bit her lip, picked up her fork and pushed a shrimp around on her plate. "I'll think about it."

"Good." Yes! Wow! She'd think about it! Progress. "And while you're there, do me a favor, okay?"

"Oh, jeez, I can't wait to hear this. What, don't wear panties and flash him?"

"Oooh, good one." Krista nodded approvingly. "No. Ask him if he has a brother."

"Why?"

"'Cause I'm seriously needing some action."

Another clatter came from the booth behind them. Its occupant leaped up. A waitress hurried over with a towel, ostensibly to mop up a spill.

Oops. Clumsy.

Krista was about to turn back to her meal when something…no, that was crazy. But yes, something…made her crane around farther for a glimpse of the man's face at the same time his eyes made the trip to visit hers.

Eureka.

Tall, not dark but handsome, yessss, and the kind of kapow chemistry that didn't happen very often but always, in her experience, promised something good. And did he look familiar? Maybe. Not quite. Most likely looked like someone else she knew.

Happiness.

"Water jump out of your glass?" She smiled and checked discreetly for a ring, hoping, when she found none, that her eyes were broadcasting the invitation she wanted them to be and that he'd respond. Because quite frankly all this talk of fantasy and thrills and the excitement of someone new had put her in the mood for her own adventure. Not to mention that she'd spend the next few days researching romantic holiday getaways without so much as the hint of a romance in her own life.

So how 'bout it, sailor?

Her sailor gave her a tight smile, threw a few bills on his table and walked past, then out of the restaurant, clearly destined for other, much luckier, ports than hers.

But she couldn't shake the strange feeling that either she'd seen that man before…or that she'd see him someday again. Soon.

3

"YOU WHAT?" SETH ROSE out of his office chair, phone to his ear, trying to tell himself he hadn't just heard what he'd heard from the lips of his stepsister. "You *what?*"

"I told you." Aimee used her snippiest pouty voice, which meant she knew she'd screwed up big-time, but rather than admit it, she'd cement herself into her own version of what was right, and not even the jackhammer of logic could cut her out of it. "I sent Juice after Krista Marlow, to the hotel you said she was going to in Maine."

"I told you that so you'd relax knowing she was out of your hair for a few days. Not so you'd send your bodyguard to beat her up." He slumped back into his father's chair. Giuseppe "Juice" Viegro—hired by Aimee a year ago after a creepy middle-aged man decided she'd been put on Earth to earn his love—could intimidate a sumo wrestler.

"You saw what she wrote about me. She thinks I'm some no-talent moron. Well, I'm not taking it anymore. She needs to understand what she writes about me hurts. And if Juice can intimidate her a little in the process, then I say good! She deserves it."

"Aimee." He used his patient-yet-threatening big-brother voice. "Does the word *harassment* mean anything to you?"

"Whadya think she's doing to *me?*"

"It's her job to write articles." He closed his eyes, shutting out the portrait of his father on the dark wood wall, holding the Wellington crest as if he was lord of the manor.

"Well, it's Juice's job to protect me and that's what he's doing."

"How is he protecting you in Maine?" Seth opened his eyes and turned his back on the portrait. His father and stepmother had raised Aimee to be this way; Seth shouldn't have to play cleanup.

"He's the only one I trust. He won't hurt her, he'll just talk to her and make her see it my way."

"Why not pay her a nice threatening visit closer to home?"

"Juice's family is in Maine. He volunteered when he saw how upset I was. I thought it was sweet of him."

"*Sweet* of him?" He clamped his lips together so he wouldn't say the word that came to mind instead of *sweet*. Juice might be enormous and terrifying, but he obviously fit just fine around Aimee's little finger. "Call him off, Aimee. Now. If he so much as touches her, even just to scare her, we could have a lawsuit on our hands so big it would—"

"I'm not calling him off. You've done nothing. It's up to me now."

"*Aimee.*"

"No." She hung up the phone, a toddler throwing a toy, a preteen stamping her foot.

Seth roared so loudly his grandmotherly and extremely efficient secretary, Sheila Bradstone, came to the door and asked him if he was all right. He blinked at her, undoubtedly bright red with fury, clutching his cell phone as if he'd like to hurl it through his corner-office window, kept frighteningly clean by the nightly janitorial crew.

"Fine." He managed a clenched-teeth smile. "Just a tad frustrated. Anything I can do for you?"

"Now that you mention it, I'm ordering Christmas gifts for the board members and wondered if you wanted me to take care of your family gifts again this year."

He resisted groaning. Since his mom had died and the warm traditions of his childhood died with her, holidays had become just another pain-in-the-ass obligation. "Sure, thanks. Whatever I got them is fine again. In a different color or something. Use your judgment."

She gave him a maternal look of concern. "Aimee causing trouble again?"

"What else?"

Sheila shook her gray head and tsk-tsked sympathetically. She'd lived through the battles Seth had getting Aimee to agree to be spokesperson for Wellington in the first place. "If she'd been my daughter…"

Seth laughed, albeit grimly, at the mental picture of Sheila taking a belt to Aimee's backside. His stepmother had no time for discipline, too busy spending Wellington money as fast as his financially conservative father let her get her hands on it. "I wish she *had* been your daughter. Then I wouldn't be at risk of developing ulcers."

"If you'll excuse me…" Sheila hesitated, frowning slightly. Which could only mean she had some opinion she was pretty sure he wasn't going to like.

"Yes?"

"Behavior like Aimee's is often a cry for attention."

"Attention?" He shook his head in disbelief. "She doesn't get enough attention from fans and her bodyguard and the press and hangers-on and—"

"Not from her family."

He sighed. Possible. But Seth was only a stepbrother, and he and Aimee had never been close. In addition, he had no time for nurturing a spoiled twenty-one-year-old kid. That was his father's job and his stepmother's—if they'd ever care to do it.

"You could be right. But if I haul out the mop and bucket every time she makes a mess, how is she going to learn to clean it up herself?"

Except this time there were others who didn't deserve to be soiled. Like Krista, in spite of what Aimee saw as justifiable provocation. And the Wellington stores. And him.

"Also a good point." Sheila clucked sympathetically and withdrew. One of the things he liked so much about her. She said her piece and shut up. A lot of women could learn from her example. Like Aimee. And Krista.

He briefly replayed the punch of attraction he felt when their eyes met at Thai Banquet, after he'd knocked over his water like a complete ass. But what man could hear an attractive woman admit to needing sex and remain unmoved? Smart, passionate and sexually open, with an invitation in her eyes that still haunted him—Krista had definitely made an impression, about as far from the one he'd expected as she could get.

Which was why he'd hightailed it out of the restaurant before he did something stupider than spilling his water, like stopping to chat her up. Once she found out he was Seth Wellington, the invitation would be to his own hanging.

So. He glanced at his watch. He had a meeting in half an hour with his hostile, old-fashioned board and George, the head buyer, brilliant at what he did but about as far out of the closet as they came, which meant an hour and a half of exhausting damage control and diplomacy for Seth, similar to what he'd gone through when he'd fired the company's stodgy advertising agency and brought in a fresh, young batch of talent.

On top of that, Aimee in her infinite generosity, had handed him a situation more potentially damaging than any of Krista's posts ever had been, one for which no immediate solution came to mind.

So. Start with the facts.

One: Giuseppi "Juice" Viegro was at this moment pursuing Ms. Krista Marlow up to the Pine Tree Inn, two states away, where Seth Wellington had been idiotic enough to mention to Aimee she was planning a visit.

Two: The only person who could call off Juice was Aimee, who apparently had no intention of doing so.

Three: Aimee's tantrums lasted approximately two days to a week, after which time she could generally be coaxed back into her usual cheerful borderline sanity.

Four: He did not have two days to a week.

Five: The police might be able to stop Juice, but not without risking unpleasant publicity, and he had no favors to call in with any law enforcement in Maine.

Six: He was screwed.

Less than three weeks to the grand opening, featuring commercials starring Aimee's lovely brunette head, and she was trying her hardest to cause him a premature heart attack.

Possible solution: Leave it alone, hope for the best and assume the worst wouldn't happen.

But…there was the image of Juice's huge build threatening Krista Marlow's tiny body, which brought on a surprising rush of outrage and protectiveness.

No way. He glanced at his watch and eyed the threatening sky to the west. Snow predicted for the evening, the first big storm of the season, sixty percent chance, too much to risk.

But…there were those vibrant blue eyes meeting his at Thai Banquet, the shock of his own powerful attraction reflected in equal measure. And the fun he'd had today when he threw off the CEO mantle and let himself play the casual charmer, free of the mold he'd been encased in for far too long.

Ridiculous. He had too little time as it was to prepare for the upcoming meeting, let alone keep on top of running the rest of the company.

But…he had nothing scheduled after the meeting, and it being Friday, he had some leeway with his schedule this weekend.

Come on, what was he thinking? He'd get hold of Juice's family and convince someone to let Seth have access to the gentle giant's cell phone number.

Twenty minutes later, after having his every turn blocked, he admitted it wouldn't be that easy. He'd done what he could.

But…Krista Marlow was alone in a hotel room in a lodge somewhere in the wilds of Maine, desperately in need of sex, harboring a fantasy of having it anonymously within minutes of meeting a stranger she was attracted to.

Someone please stop him thinking what he was thinking.

He could stay here and pretend none of it was happening, leave Aimee to clean up her own mess, as he felt she should.

Or…

He could go after Juice…and maybe Krista…himself.

"HOW ABOUT THAT DRINK?"

Lucy nearly dropped the file she was about to put away. "Oh. Josh. Hi."

She made herself look nonchalantly into his dark eyes and told her heart to calm the hell down. New toy. Shiny toy. Not better than what she had at home, just different.

"Did you forget?"

She made herself laugh, mind racing. Forget the possibility of going out with him? Uh, no. But she couldn't do this. Could she? Was she going to do this? Krista would say she had to.

"No, I didn't forget."

He sat on the edge of her desk and tipped his head, watching her. His eyes were so, so dark. "And…do you want to go?"

Yes. God, yes. With a sudden force that shocked the hell out of her, she wanted to.

"My boyfriend. Link. I don't think he'd…" She gestured stupidly back and forth between herself and Josh.

"This isn't about Link."

She flashed him a warning glance and he put up both hands in surrender. He had nice hands, narrower than Link's and with longer fingers. "Don't get me wrong. I'm a nice guy. I'm not out to make you do anything you don't want to. And I'm not trying to bust anything up, especially if he makes you happy."

Her head started spinning. She took her time tucking the holiday party file back in its place in her desk drawer, wishing he hadn't phrased it quite that way. *Especially if he makes you happy.* "Thank you."

"But unless I'm wrong here, and you can feel free to tell me if I am…"

His silence made her look up again. Her stomach-flipping reaction to his obvious concern made her wish she hadn't. "Yes?"

"You don't strike me as happy."

She bent her head, closed the drawer. "Things are… tough right now."

Oh, good one, Lucy. Open the door and invite a man you're madly attracted to right into your vulnerability and confusion. Call her the queen of earnestly blundering into stupid situations. Too much honesty was not a good thing. Especially around someone she had no real relationship with.

"I'm a good listener." He smiled. Even his teeth were perfect. He looked like a movie star, like a rougher, more masculine version of Orlando Bloom but with that same slender, dark-curled, dreamy perfection. "And I'm good at meaningless chatter if you don't feel like talking about anything intense."

"Why do you want to go out with me?"

He gave a little shake of his head as if he couldn't believe she'd ask such a question. "Because I like you. I don't get to talk to you much at work. You're always so serious and I have a feeling there's a lot more to you than this. A lot more."

Whoa. His voice had dropped to a husky, seductive murmur on the last three words. She could barely breathe from the excitement of a man so intrigued by her. This was getting very, very dangerous.

Link. She loved Link. This guy was cotton-candy fluff and Link was the salt of her earth.

"Link and I are—"

"This has nothing to do with you and Link. I'm after friendship." He looked pained for a second, then slid off her desk and crossed to the empty couch where people sat waiting to see her boss, Alexis. "Okay, maybe that's bullshit. Maybe I just want it to be true because it would be easier. But if friendship is all you have to offer me, I'll take it, Lucy."

Her name came off his tongue, traveled across the room and sounded like the best thing she'd ever heard.

"I don't know what to say."

He turned and met her eyes, grinned, slow and lazy and sexier than was good for her sanity. "That's better than no."

She cleared her throat. Link was home waiting for her. There was no way she could do this to him. "I'm afraid no is all I can say right now."

"Right now?" He crossed the room back to her and she dropped her eyes, unable to take the hope in his.

She should say *or ever.* She needed to say it. She *had* to say it. Or she'd open up such a Pandora's box she'd never be safe again. Never again feel the world belonged only to Link and her. If she let this man in…

God, she wanted to.

"Maybe…a drink would be okay. Sometime."

"Not today?"

"No. I can't. I have to—" She looked at her watch, trying to think of something besides *get home to Link and cook his dinner,* because that made her sound so dull and slavish. "Go. Somewhere."

Yeah, quick thinking, Lucy. She was no good at lying. She'd be no good at cheating.

"Okay." He smiled and touched her shoulder the way a friend might, just a gentle tap. Only it didn't affect her the way a friend's touch would. "I'm really looking forward to 'sometime.'"

She watched him walk away, his smooth, graceful stride so different from Link's powerful, lumbering step, and sank back into her chair, cheeks on fire. What had she done?

And what was she going to do with the terrible fear that he wasn't looking forward to "sometime" even half as much as she was?

KRISTA PEERED THROUGH her snow-shrunk windshield, wipers clearing the white fluff away as fast as it could fall. And it was falling fast. Good thing she'd gotten restless and left earlier than she'd planned this afternoon. She was a few miles from the inn and the snow had only been falling for an hour or so, but the radio report indicated travel conditions were going to get worse as the evening wore on.

At least the drive had been lovely. She'd been to Maine quite a few times but never stopped being amazed at the change from the New Hampshire border, across the Piscataqua River, into the peace and green of the appropriately nicknamed Pine Tree State. This time she'd traveled farther north than the usual coastal hotels and shopping meccas. She'd left 95 at Route 201, the Old Canada Road National Scenic Byway, and headed northwest to Skowhegan. Then past. Then after forever, she'd turned onto what was a fairly unpromising-looking little track, which Betty Robinson, the Pine Tree Inn owner, had cheerfully assured her was not going to seem right but was.

If she said so.

Certainly no problems with traffic. Maine was not jammed this time of year as it could be in summer. Ideal for what Krista was after. Off-the-beaten-track romantic holiday getaways.

So far she could see how this could be very romantic. Closer to Skowhegan there had been other choices, one inn in particular had caught her eye online while planning this trip—king-size beds and fireplaces in every room. But she was determined to stay away from the usual destinations, so here she was, miles from a town of any size, bumping through the snow to the Pine Tree Inn, frankly unsure of what to expect....

And wishing she wasn't alone. Thinking—for no good reason and in spite of having told herself a thousand times to stop—of a pair of hazel eyes recently sighted in a Thai restaurant and wishing they were along for the ride. Then this visit could have been the romantic launch to a new adventure, which maybe *this time* would have worked out forever.

Or at least longer than a-few-to-several weeks.

Total attraction. Unbelievable attraction. Nearly unbearable attraction.

Wistful sigh.

Had he responded to her amazing charms and inviting smile by walking forward, grabbing her arms, hoisting her to her feet, gazing into her eyes while breath swelled his manly chest and declared he'd never felt such a pull to any woman before and would she please accompany him to the nearest spot where they could get comfortable and privately and immediately naked or he'd go mad from wanting?

Um. No.

He'd missed most of her inviting smile and obviously had no problem dismissing her amazing charms, because after that breath-stealing connection, he couldn't get away from her fast enough.

Not that it was necessarily about her. Maybe he really was in a crazed hurry to leave, and maybe he regretted walking away from what might have been as much as she regretted him walking.

But then maybe Lucy was right, and Krista was too into the hot bod and the hot chemistry and maybe she should start dating men she wasn't that attracted to. Men she could feel so-so about while insisting she was in love, hanging on year in and out, after anything they had in common had long since fled screaming from the boredom. Just like Lucy.

Good idea!

Not.

She'd a thousand times rather suffer through one passionate relationship after another exploding into shrapnel than hang on to the safe but mediocre for fear of being alone.

Though just once she'd really like to get it right, without the explosion, at least not so damn soon after the fun started.

Another mile through ever-thickening snow and the road widened into an empty parking area—was she the only guest here?—with tiny cabins barely visible through the white whirl, the closest with a red Office sign hanging beside the door and Christmas lights glowing blurry green along the eaves.

Krista parked and uncramped her fingers from the wheel, stretched and rolled her shoulders. She'd made it. And with the fat flakes falling as fast as possible, not a moment too soon.

Door open, she stepped into the crunching snow, already accumulated to over an inch, and pulled out her overnight bag, glad she'd worn boots just in case. A mug of hot decaf would taste fabulous right now, and she looked forward to a chat with the owners about annual holiday events in the surrounding area, to flesh out her article.

Unfortunately chatting would have to be done another time. A black-and-white Closed sign hung in the office window under an envelope with her name on it taped to the glass and another one above it that read "Smith." Great. Not only was she the only guest, the place was entirely deserted of staff, too. Who knew if this Smith person would even show up, considering the weather.

Hmm.

She did a slow three-sixty, taking in the darkening sky, the wind picking up.

Romantic? Or creepy?

For a second, the idea of driving back into Skowhegan appealed. Until she realized she'd have to drive through worsening snow, which could become not only an annoyance but a serious hazard on unfamiliar roads. And she'd have wasted the chance to write this article, which could become a humor piece if need be: Romantic-Getaways Author Becomes Stephen King Heroine.

Only, in case the fates were feeling tempted, she was kidding about the horror stuff.

Kidding.

She shivered, grabbed the envelope and ripped it open. Two keys—thank goodness they'd honored that request. She'd locked herself out of too many hotel rooms to count and asked for an extra as a matter of routine now. On each key ring hung a small, rough wooden circle, the cross-section of a tree branch with distinctive white birch bark still

clinging in places. The circles had the cabin numbers
burned into them. She peered at the first. Cabin six.
Frowned at the second. Unless she was mistaken, the other
key had a nine on it, though it was hard to tell, the way
the wooden disks spun. Someone must have picked them
up in a hurry, not realizing one was upside down.

Nice. Though considering the weather, no chance of
her coming outside to get locked out in the first place.
Not as if there was a lot of nightlife in the area to be
explored…except maybe animal.

Krista glanced around nervously through the white at
more white-covered shapes. Trying to feel like a brave ad-
venturess instead of a city girl tossed to the wolves, she
made her way to cabin six and tried both keys. The six key
worked, the nine definitely didn't. Oh, well. She was only
here one night then, weather permitting, on to a B and B
in Jackman tomorrow. Having only one working key
wasn't going to be a problem.

She pushed inside and flipped on the light, relieved to
be out of the snow but surprised not to be enveloped in a
rush of warm air. Maybe they left the cabins unheated until
the guests arrived to save fuel? Understandable, but chilling. As was the total silence. She prowled around, hyper-
conscious of every bump, swish and creak of her steps,
taking in the cold-but-cozy feel of the place—a bit too log
cabin and geometric Native American for her taste, but
then if a lot of their guests were hunters, she couldn't exactly expect floral and froufrou.

There was a gas fireplace on the right, at the foot of the
king-size bed. On a table to the left sat a potted miniature
Christmas tree, three wrapped fresh-looking blueberry
muffins, boxes of cold cereal and—thank goodness—a

coffeepot with several packs of good coffee and tiny tubs of half-and-half. A mini refrigerator held glass bottles of premium orange juice and single-serving cartons of milk. The spotless bathroom had a large tub and a small basket with shampoo, conditioner and lotion.

Not half bad for less than fifty dollars a night. Very nice, in fact.

But unless she had less than the sense she was born with, no thermostat. No heating unit against the wall. So the fireplace must be it. How cozy. *And* romantic! She swooped over to it and searched for the controls. Exactly the warming touch the room needed, figuratively and literally.

Except, after a good half hour of frustrated attempts, finally using the last match in the box she'd dug out of her purse, she couldn't get the damn thing to work. As far as she could tell, no gas was flowing at all.

She picked up the room phone and left a message with the office, though chances were with the storm raging, no one would be making the rounds tonight.

Irritation.

Thank God it was in the thirties and not single digits. She'd brought her new warm flannel nightgown instead of the one washed thin, and in a king bed the blankets could be doubled over onto one side. For internal heat, the coffeemaker could make decaf, and she always had herbal-tea packets in her purse.

She'd be okay. This would be an adventure, in fact. Right? Her article would be funny and charming. Single woman's attempt to stay warm on lonely night in romantic cabin.

Very lonely.

She changed into her nightgown and brushed her teeth, starting to shiver. Except for the occasional wind gust or creaking branch, the silence was absolute—that particular dead silence of a snowy evening. Even cities grew quiet, muffled, when the lovely white blanket dropped. Though here, instead of cars picking their way cautiously through the snow, she could all too easily picture moose and bear nosing around the cabin in the darkness.

Gulp. Good thing she slept with earplugs or she'd imagine the great beasts pawing and snuffling to get in no matter what she heard.

Of course, bears and moose sounded pretty tame once you started imagining forest-dwelling psychos investigating apparently deserted hotels. Drunk. High. Armed.

Not going to think about that.

Not.

She slid into bed, unwilling to stay out in the chill long enough to do her Yoga routine—it was hard to relax when your teeth were chattering. The sheets were icy at first, but gradually her body heat and the huge pile of blankets started a slow, lovely thaw, which changed the icebox into a deliciously warm cocoon. Better with company, but mmm, nice. Maybe she'd start turning off the radiators in her apartment at night, too. Maybe that article would come out just fine.

She yawned and blinked a few times, then closed her eyes, trying to clear her mind, fill it with peace and calm and warm golden light instead of images of the vast woods around her and things that go bump in the night and the fact that no one could hear her scream.

Mostly she'd keep at bay the fact that during this off-the-beaten-track romantic getaway research trip, she had absolutely no hope of romance.

4

HE SHOULD BE FURIOUS.

Seth Wellington IV should be ragingly furious. He should be railing at Aimee, cursing Juice, hauling out his cell to hurl orders at his secretary, Sheila, and generally making life miserable for as many people as possible, which was what pissed-off CEOs were best at.

Most of all he should be annoyed at himself for wasting time going on this ridiculous wild-goose chase into the middle of absolutely freaking nowhere in a blinding snowstorm when he had about a million other things he should be doing.

Instead he was loving it. The perfect errand for a man who must be every kind of fool to be on it.

The second he'd crossed the bridge into Maine, leaving behind beautiful but industrial Portsmouth, New Hampshire, and entered the vast peaceful expanse of pine forest, he'd known he'd been away too damn long. Maine never failed to feed his soul. And judging from the way he'd rolled down his windows and gleefully gulped familiar lungfuls of the cold, damp, pine-scented air, his soul had been starving.

That it was insanity to go on this trip he didn't question. That he felt saner than he had in way too long was something that needed closer inspection....

When he wasn't trying so hard to stay on the road.

Krista hadn't been kidding about the off-the-beaten-track part. He'd been to Skowhegan before, to the state fair, but not beyond the town. His travels in Maine had been primarily coastal. He'd stayed way up the coast near the Canadian border a whole summer, longer than he'd stayed anywhere else on his trip. The life, the smells, the atmosphere, the old man he'd gotten to know better than anyone during his year-plus of travel, all had found a place in his heart and all had been nearly forgotten until his return today.

But, of course, this time he was, as always, operating on short notice and a tight schedule. The whole way from Boston he'd kept an eye out for Juice's hideously over-detailed red Camaro and come up empty—not that he thought it likely he'd find that needle in this highway haystack. Seth had called Aimee several time to see if she'd heard anything, but Her Poutiness refused to take his call.

And Sheila wondered why he didn't like dealing with his stepsister any more than he had to?

He found a gap in the woods that fit the description of the road the inn owners told him to look for and took the turn slowly, following the flat white track through the trees, which theoretically would lead him to the Pine Tree Inn. He damn well hoped so. The gas in his car would get him back to Skowhegan to fill up in the morning but not a hell of a lot farther. He couldn't afford to be wandering lost in the Maine woods.

The thought startled him. Since when? Years back he would have relished such an adventure. If he'd run out of gas, he would have slept in his car or found a way to make a shelter and find food, thrilled at being so directly in touch with basic survival instincts. Times like that brought a man closer to the essence of being human.

Hint: It had nothing to do with corporate merchandising.

So he'd grown soft again.

Well that was life. When you were sure fate would lead in the direction you needed to go to learn the most, it took a sharp U-turn and taught you something else. This trip tonight had made him realize all the more how far he'd strayed from the person he thought he'd become. Chasing after Aimee's screwup had already managed to be a lot more worthwhile than he'd expected—and there was still more to come.

Though he really didn't want to arrive at the inn and find Juice there causing Krista any trouble. Unfortunately since Juice had a head start on both Seth and the snow, that was the most likely scenario. Then what? At worst, confrontation or hostility from Juice. Confrontation and hostility from Krista was probably given, but he had more confidence in his ability to handle her. Seth was no wimp, but Juice was…enormous. And as a bodyguard, probably trained in violent confrontation. Comforting thought.

Seth's Camry jolted and slipped over what was probably a rock in the road, and he found himself gripping the wheel too tightly. No point focusing on the worst. At best, if Juice had arrived, there would be awkwardness and confusion. He liked that version a lot better.

If Seth had his way, Juice would have given up his quest, cancelled it due to weather and gone straight to visit his folks in Waterville. Because neither Seth's best- nor worst-case scenario would look good when the full report appeared in a savage satire on Krista's blog. Maybe not such a problem now, but in two weeks when the stores' new direction became public, reporters would dig up the story. Newspapers would feast on a tale of conflict and scandal and revenge....

Seth shuddered, then forced himself to relax. No point worrying now. Juice was the unknown quantity; Seth couldn't claim to have a close personal relationship with Aimee's cherished protection. He could only hope the giant would listen to reason. Or at least that Aimee would take a call from Juice, then let Seth talk her into backing off.

He jostled around a curve and, miracle of miracles, there it was. The Pine Tree Inn, with, thank God, only one snow-covered car in the parking lot—not a red Camaro. Either Juice had already come and gone—and Seth didn't at *all* like the idea of Krista alone and scared or worse after his visit—or he'd never made it this far. Maybe Aimee *had* called him off and let Seth keep going out of spite. He wouldn't put it past her. Possibly Juice had been delayed by the snow and would still arrive sometime later tonight, though with the weather this bad, it was unlikely he'd keep trying. Even Seth, experienced in winter driving, had been fleetingly tempted to stay in Skowhegan.

He pulled out his cell and dialed Aimee again. Again she didn't pick up, but he left another message, telling her he was at the Pine Tree Inn, that he'd talk to Ms. Marlow on Aimee's behalf and that she better call Juice off or risk a hell of a lot worse publicity than Krista had ever exposed her to.

Then he hung up and laughed incredulously, shaking his head. A screwed-up situation, but he'd done what he could. If Juice showed up later tonight, at least Seth had gotten here first and could sort things out. If Juice didn't show up…

A glance out through the snow at the cabins. Krista was in one of them. Was she thinking about her fantasy tonight?

He rubbed his fingers back and forth over his chin, then yanked his brain back from of his own fantasy. Right. Krista would really be turned on seeing a guy she'd smiled at in a restaurant three states away show up a day later in a secluded cabin trying to seduce her. If she had a weapon, he wouldn't blame her for using it first, asking questions later.

Out of the car, bag slung over his shoulder, he trudged through the deepening snow, yawning and swinging his arms. He was tired, it was getting late and he needed a bathroom, a cuppa and a bed.

Taped to the office door, as Betty Robinson had said it would be, was the envelope bearing the name Smith. He tore it open and took out the key. Cabin six.

A few minutes spent trudging through thick blowing snow and he figured out which was cabin six. The key went in and turned smoothly; he shut the door quickly behind to keep the storm from—

His instincts went from zero to sixty in no seconds.

What the—

There wasn't much light in the cabin at all. A gold sliver on the floor from the bulb left burning in the bathroom. But there was enough. Enough to see that the lone bed in the room was occupied.

Krista? He took a few steps toward the bed and waited, letting his eyes get used to the dimness. The figure on the bed turned.

Krista. It had to be.

What the hell was she doing in his cabin?

For a crazy instant he imagined her engineering the shared room to make her fantasy come true. Just as quickly he realized that was impossible.

So…was he in *her* cabin? Had Betty Robinson left him the wrong damn key? Or left Krista the wrong one? Had Betty gotten confused and thought he and Krista were together?

This was nuts. Where could he go now? He had no other key, there was no one at the office, the weather sucked, no other place to stay for miles around and he was nearly out of gas—figuratively when it came to his body and literally when it came to his car.

He was stuck.

For crying out loud, this was…it was completely… totally…entirely…

Hmm…

Interesting.

A red-blooded male and a hot-blooded female trapped anonymously in the middle of nowhere in the middle of a snowstorm in the middle of a dark, cozy cabin.

Well.

He could think of one or two immediate consequences to this situation that could be extremely pleasant. As long as they left whatever might happen between them in the fantasy realm Krista spoke of. The reality of who they were and why they'd been brought together was best left far, far out of the picture—and the bedroom—for both their sakes.

A tantalizing thought.

Either way, he'd have to wake her and let her know he was here without telling her who he was and—far trickier—tell her that he was staying until morning. Or until the snow stopped. Or both.

How to wake her without scaring her to death? He took a step closer, eyes adjusting to the darkness, and thought he glimpsed the bright orange foam of plugs in her ears. Not that she needed them in this blissful, far-reaching quiet; she most likely slept with them out of habit.

That was good. He could at least use the bathroom and figure out what to do while he warmed up.

Except now that he thought about it, there didn't seem to be warming up happening. Why hadn't she turned up the heat? Hell, he didn't think she'd even turned *on* the heat.

He shrugged, used the bathroom as quietly as possible, holding his breath until the water stopped running, anticipating a female scream of terror any second.

Nothing.

A peek into the room—half expecting her to be hovering outside the door, wielding a baseball bat or worse—he found her still sleeping. Seth breathed yet another sigh of relief, washed his face and brushed his teeth. Turned out the bathroom light, took off his sweater and boots and laid them in a neat pile next to his bag.

He was ready. If she wouldn't let him share her bed in whatever capacity, he'd steal half the blankets and bunk on the floor. No way was he going back out there and freezing to death just to be a gentleman.

A few strides over toward her, feeling keyed-up, nervous, keyed-up. Did he mention keyed-up?

"Hey. Hello."

She didn't move. He took a step closer. Another one. "Hey."

Nothing. For all his adventures around the country, he had no experience waking women in the middle of the night and announcing he intended to stay. What would be least scary for someone sleeping in a silent, locked cabin with every expectation of being alone for the entire night—to be woken with a soft voice? A gentle touch? Or not woken at all until she rolled over and encountered an unexpected bedmate?

Probably not the third. He didn't know. Maybe a combination of the first and second. He moved around to the empty side of the bed, sat on the edge and put his hand on her shoulder.

"Hey," he whispered. "Sleeping beauty, wake up."

Her eyes shot open. She yelled, lunged away in terror, her progress hampered by the huge pile of bedcovers over her.

"Get away from me. Get away." She flailed at him, tore out her earplugs and swung again with her fists, trying to kick at him through the mound of blankets and quilts.

"It's okay." He grabbed her wrists, pinned them to the bed to save his jaw and head from punches aimed with the strength of panic, aware that pinning her down was only going to frighten her more. This was insane. How had he thought this could turn into a sexy fantasy? This was every woman's nightmare. "I'm not going to hurt you, I swear."

She gave a short animal scream of frustration and fear, unable to free herself, panting and struggling.

"I'm not a criminal, I'm a totally normal guy who got the key to your cabin by mistake." He spoke loudly enough for her to hear but slowly, patiently and as reassuringly as he could, cursing the need for the darkness that must make him shadowy and frightening. But with lights on, if she recognized him from the restaurant, he'd scare her even more. If she recognized him as Seth Wellington... He couldn't even think about that. "I'm not going to hurt you. Do you understand?"

She nodded, breath rasping in her throat, emitting gasps and an occasional hoarse moan that sent chills across his neck. He never, ever wanted to hear anything like that fear again.

"I'm not going to hurt you. The owners of the inn, the Robinsons, left me the key to your cabin by mistake. I woke you so you'd know I was here. Do you understand?"

She nodded again, still breathing harshly, then worked her mouth a couple of times until the word came out. "Smith?"

Smith… The lightbulb clicked on. "Yes. That's me. They left me the wrong key at the office. I got yours by mistake, came in and found you in what I thought was my bed."

Her breathing slowed down. "The envelope…on the door."

"Right."

She inhaled long and exhaled longer, her body relaxing slightly, which called his attention to the fact that it was dark and they were both in the same bed and he was still pinning her down and that she was sexy as hell, even frightened.

Great, he got off on scaring women.

No. He got off on Krista Marlow in bed in the dark.

"You scared me to death, Smith."

"I'm sorry." His voice came out lower than it needed to and he cleared his throat. "I couldn't think of any other way."

"Cabin nine," she whispered.

"Sorry?"

"They gave me two keys. They must have mixed up six and nine, and given you my second key. I always ask for two."

"Why?"

"So I don't get locked out. And so I don't have to break

into strangers' rooms and attempt to stop their hearts from fear." She let out a few more short breaths. "I still have enough adrenaline going to win a marathon."

"I'm sorry." He found himself wanting to smile. A sense of humor in a bad situation. He liked that. "If I let go of your hands, will you try to brain me again?"

"No."

"Because you trust me now?"

"No."

He wanted to smile again in spite of the fact that she sounded dead serious. "But I'm supposed to trust that you won't go for my eyeballs if I let your hands go?"

"All I can give you is my word."

"I gave you mine."

She snorted. "But you broke into my cabin."

"I walked in with the key they left me."

She moved restlessly and he had to keep himself from trying to make out the lines of her body against the sheets. Apparently he was an unprincipled pervert.

"I…won't hit you."

"Why not, if you don't trust me?"

"I don't know. I probably should hit you. But I won't."

He stared down at her dim shape, knowing he was stalling but reluctant to release her. Because then he might have to take the correct key and leave her warm bed and her even warmer body and the sweet powdery scent of her. "Promise?"

"Yes. I promise." Her voice dropped to a husky murmur and he started to get hard. He didn't release her but eased his grip enough so she could slip her hands free with little effort.

She hesitated, and for one cock-jumping moment he

thought she wasn't going to move. He heard her swallow in the darkness, then felt her hands slide slowly until they were just free of his but lay still on the mattress on either side of her head, close enough that he could move his thumbs and stroke her palms if the urge struck.

The urge was definitely striking—but her earlier fear stopped him. He was a stranger. Maybe her fantasy stranger, but until she trusted him or gave him a go-ahead sign, he couldn't act on his attraction.

"Where is the key?" In spite of his noble thoughts, he barely got the words out.

"Oh...the key. There." She twisted her head and pointed to the table beside her bed, then lay back, looking up at him, waiting for what he'd do next.

He knew what he wanted to do next. There was no doubt at all what he wanted to do next. He wanted to lower his mouth and taste her skin, taste her mouth, stoke the chemistry between them until it was too hot to do anything but give in.

But he couldn't risk freaking her out again. The sounds of her fear were too raw and too recent.

At the same time, he wasn't jumping for the key and leaving either, was he. "Why don't you have the heat on?"

"There is no heat. And I couldn't get the fireplace going."

"It's damn chilly in here."

"No kidding." She laughed, slightly breathless, and he realized how much he wanted her to say, *Can I warm you up?* "That's why I have on every possible layer of blankets, doubled."

"Bet it's warm in there at least."

"Were you hoping I'd invite you in?" Her tone was sharp, but he sensed no real bite.

"Absolutely." She tensed and he made himself chuckle, knowing he should shut up and stop leaning so closely over her. "I was kidding."

She tilted her head, a dark outline gazing up at him from her pillow. "Why aren't you getting the key?"

"I don't know." That much was the truth. "Why aren't I?"

"I don't know. You're sure you're not a stalking, murdering sex offender?"

"Not last time I checked." He lingered a beat longer, then pushed regretfully to sitting upright. Sex with Krista right now was a great idea—and a bad one. She still didn't trust him entirely and he couldn't blame her. If their positions were reversed and she'd scared the hell out of him in the middle of the night, he might have a hard time swallowing the mix-up story, too.

He stood and reached over to the table beside her bed, located the key and squinted at the wooden ring. Cabin nine, whadya know.

"Here's the key." He suppressed a sigh. "I guess I'll be—"

"What's your first name, Smith?"

Her voice was shy and he felt a jolt of pleasure that she'd stopped him from leaving. "John."

"John Smith? Seriously?"

"Not entirely."

"Because you're wanted by the police?"

"Because I wanted to escape reality for a while."

"Oh." She nodded and her hair made a rustling sound on the pillow. "I know what that's like."

"Yeah?" He hoped she'd go on but didn't expect it.

"My name is—"

"I know your name."

"You do?" The fear crept back into her voice.

"Jane Doe."

She laughed softly, as if afraid to make too much noise in the hushed cabin. "Exactly. Have we met before, John Smith?"

"We must have if I know your name."

Silence fell. What was she thinking? If he had his way, she was thinking that maybe her fantasy could be fulfilled right here, right now....

Then probably following that up with thinking she'd be a fool to fulfill it with someone who could end up hacking her to pieces afterward. Sociopaths gave the rest of humanity a bad name.

Unless he was totally off base and she was lying there wondering why he hadn't gotten the hell out of her cabin so she could go back to sleep.

"Thanks for the key." He stood, swinging the chain in his fingers. "I'm really sorry I scared you."

"Okay." She sat up, holding the covers to her chest. "I hope your cabin has heat."

"If it does, would you like to—"

"No. I'm fine here, thanks." She spoke quickly, then gave a small snort that sounded like disgust and mumbled something under her breath.

"What was that?"

"Oh. Just…nothing."

"Okay then, Jane Doe. Happy trails."

He picked up his bag and sweater, stepped into his boots and yanked on his coat. "Nice meeting you. Sorry for the near heart attack."

"It worked out okay."

He opened the door, squinted in anticipation of the stinging snow as he reached for the storm-door handle.

"John."

He turned back. "Yes."

The light outside spilled dimly into the room. Krista still sat on the bed, leaning on one arm by her pillow, the other still clutching covers to her chest, the languid mistress of her cabin. "Do you want to…would you mind checking the fireplace?"

He closed the door behind him, resisting the urge to smile. "Check the fireplace."

"I…couldn't get it to work."

"I see." He took off his coat again, tossed it onto a dark blob that had the shape of a chair, followed it with his sweater and stepped out of his boots. He was in. Call it instinct, call it whatever you want, but he and Krista were going to make some fantasies come true tonight. "Can't even get a spark?"

"I don't think there's any fuel running."

"And you need heat."

"Yes." Her voice dropped to a whisper. "I need heat."

He walked toward the bed, not even pretending to go near the fireplace. "I don't know much about fireplaces."

"No?"

"No." He stopped at the edge of the bed, reached and touched her hair, followed it down the line of her cheek. "But I know about generating heat."

Her breath went in, then out, and did it again—sweet, short breaths, no gasping, hoarse fear this time. "Really."

"Do you want me to show you?"

"I…think so…."

"If you say no, I'll leave. But unless I'm crazy…I don't think you want me to leave."

"No. I don't want you to leave." She laughed softly. "And I think that makes me the crazy one."

He knelt on the bed, one knee, then the other, keeping each movement slow, nonthreatening.

"We're strangers. That makes it risky for both of us." He put his hands to her shoulders, spread his fingers, feeling her small bones, then drew his hands down her arms, surprisingly firm and muscled for a woman who appeared so delicate, "Also more exciting."

"Yes." She inhaled on the word, exhaled on a quiet laugh. Nervous. Excited. Aroused.

He was, too.

He pulled her hand up to his mouth, gently tasted each fingertip. Her nails were short, blunt, the nails of a typist. He'd had his skin shredded by too many expensive talons, and the discovery turned him on. Who knew natural nails would excite him? Maybe everything about this woman would excite him. He brought her image to mind from the restaurant. Blue, vivid eyes. Blond, wispy hair. Body tiny and, as he was discovering, tough as her attitude.

But she wasn't Krista tonight. And Seth Wellington IV was somewhere else, too. His were someone else's CEO problems tonight.

Reality was safely back home in Boston.

Her arms slid up his chest. He leaned to kiss her; her lips were soft and sweet, and his nerves fled. This was right. Everything that happened between them for the rest of the night would be right, too.

Just too bad it would be right for so damn many wrong reasons.

5

KRISTA OPENED HER EYES. What had woken her? Still pitch-dark, still cold as hell in the cabin, though nice and warm under the covers. But something had...mmm, brushed her thigh. And there, again.

Fingers, if she wasn't mistaken.

Mmm.

She smiled and moved her hips in a provocative circle, eliciting a deep approving groan behind her. Her excitement rocketed to a feverish pitch. No question, but having sex with someone she'd never seen was intensely exciting. Her fantasy of immediate intimacy with a stranger had been taken to the ultimate degree—more of the unknown, more of the danger.

Yet she'd found herself willing to trust this John Smith. Maybe for no more valid reason than she wanted to. Maybe tonight that was enough. But if she hadn't finally gotten up the nerve to ask him to stay, she believed he would have left as he'd promised to. A creep wouldn't have given up so easily, especially when he'd had every advantage with her pinned helpless on the bed. He could have done anything he wanted...and he had only done his best to put her at ease.

Once that soothing, patient voice had started talking

and she'd instinctively felt he wasn't going to hurt her, it had slowly crept into her diminishing panic that her perfect fantasy had been dropped right into her lap. Nearly literally. Like a gift. The fear and the darkness, his sexy voice and the feeling that if she didn't take advantage, circumstances might never again conspire so perfectly, had fueled her arousal and her nerve until she found herself calling him back.

Those fingers found a certain lovely spot between her legs and began an expert rhythm that spread sexual heat farther through her. Oooh, that was nice. She arched, offering herself to him behind her, heard him open and extract a condom. Then he was back, the cool latex on his penis searching for entrance, waiting to be warmed by her body.

She reached down and opened herself wide, not needing any more foreplay, just wanting him inside her again. His hands felt huge controlling her hips as he found his way in; she felt tiny and helpless, impaled by her faceless lover, large and muscular and dominant behind her.

He started a slow rhythm and she pushed back against him, heard him breathe harshly from his throat, a noise she already knew was his sign of arousal. Lack of sight had heightened her other senses; she knew his shape, his taste, his textures and sounds with an acuteness she couldn't remember with any other lover.

He was clean-shaven, though stubbled now; his lips were firm and smooth, his voice deep, mature, his build impressively trim and muscled, no middle-aged spare tire.

And he loved sex as much as she did. No fumbling, no embarrassment. No shyness. No holding back. Their lovemaking had an intensity to it she'd never experienced before.

"Is that good?" He kept one hand on her hip, put the other on the back of her neck.

"Mmm, yes."

"Can you take it harder?"

"Yes."

His thrusts became quicker, more powerful. She lifted her top leg, hooked it back over his.

"Touch yourself, Jane Doe," he whispered. "Make yourself come for me."

She moaned and moved eager fingers to obey. The darkness set her free; she was ten times less inhibited with this stranger than with men she'd dated for weeks.

"Is it good?"

"Yes." She rubbed herself faster, feeling the arousal building hotter, higher. "Oh, yes."

"I wish I could see you." His hands clamped her hips; he moved harder inside her. "Am I hurting you?"

"No. No." She countered his thrusts, her own fingers stroking furiously. She'd already come twice during the night, was about to again. This was a record for her.

"Are you close?"

"Yes." She was nearly sobbing, out of her mind with excitement. "Yes. I'm close. I'm…I'm there."

He pumped harder. Her orgasm burned through her with such strength, she let out a strangled scream.

"Am I hurting you?" The strain of his excitement cut his words sharp and short.

"No. Don't stop." She could lie there forever feeling him take his pleasure, rough and hard with her body, giving as much as he took. Her orgasm receded, but the arousal stayed high, anticipating the thrill of his climax.

She didn't have to wait long. He moaned low in his

throat, the breath rasped out and he finished inside her with long thrusts that set off waves of intense pleasure-pain.

Oh, my word. She, Krista, independent, driven, strong woman, got off as she'd never gotten off before on being dominated by a macho stranger in the dark.

She came down slowly, her body still warm and glowing, feeling a sudden emotional ache she didn't want to be feeling. Perfect sex, that was it. Deal with it.

His hand ran down her back, a lazy, meandering caress. He pulled out carefully, disposed of the condom, then hugged her back to him. "Hey, you okay?"

"Yes." Had he picked up on her mood change in the dark?

"I was pretty rough. You sure?"

"I loved it."

She didn't know you could hear someone smile, but she heard him. He caressed gently up and down her abdomen, into the curls between her legs where her swollen sex still throbbed, then back up, his huge hands deliciously warm on her breasts. "Sorry I woke you again."

"Not me."

He chuckled and she surprised herself by twisting around to give him two hard, passionate kisses on his gorgeous mouth, all she'd allow herself. Kisses outside of sex were intimate, loving, sweet exchanges. That didn't belong here tonight, though she couldn't help stealing those.

"Go back to sleep."

She smiled. It was going to take her racing heart a long time to slow enough for sleep; her racing brain even longer...

"I'm too revved up."

"Hmm, why would that be?"

"I think my orgasm broke the sound barrier. Tomorrow

all the trees around the cabin will have been felled by shock waves."

He chuckled again, squeezed her affectionately. And because she was a sop, she found herself beaming at the thought that he got her humor and maybe liked her as well as lusted.

As if it made the slightest difference for what they needed from each other tonight.

"We also need to check for cracks in the forest floor. I think mine caused an earthquake."

She laughed, a too-loud sound in the darkness. "Lucky we're so far from civilization."

"True. We wouldn't want deaths on our hands."

"Or the resulting lawsuits."

She lay in the comfortable silence, savoring the feel of being entwined with a warm male body. Some women seemed able to jump from long-term relationship to long-term relationship. Krista had never managed to do that and she wasn't sure why. So when she got these pockets of physical contact, of the wonderful deep peace and security of being in a man's arms, she always concentrated hard on every aspect so she could call it up again when she was back home.

Though she had a feeling she'd miss more than this man's arms.

Her throat tightened at the thought of this adventure being over. What was the matter with her?

"So answer me this, Jane Doe."

She forced a grin he couldn't see. "What's a nice girl like me doing in a place like this?"

"Sure, if you want to tell."

"Research."

"For *Penthouse?*"

Her laughter rang out again. "Not quite. Places couples can go to escape Christmas insanity."

"You go insane every year?"

"Doesn't everyone? Though actually not me so much. I celebrate with my family. We have pretty calm traditions."

"Tell me."

Krista wrinkled her nose. Sharing family Christmas traditions wasn't part of her sexual fantasy. She could jokingly tell him she liked to do three men dressed as Santa all at once, but something about him made her want to give him a straight answer. "We all make Christmas Eve dinner together, drinking sherry, which I think most of us hate, my sister's boyfriend most of all, but it's a tradition by now. You know how that is?"

"Sure." He responded quietly, respectfully, and her courage grew.

"Then we sing carols around the fireplace in the living room. My sister plays the piano." She raised up, wishing she could see him more clearly, touched that he hadn't made fun of their celebration. "I guess it sounds hokey."

"Not at all. My mom and I made hot buttered rum and popcorn and watched *The Grinch Who Stole Christmas,* like we used to when I was a kid."

"You drank rum when you were a kid?"

"Milk and cookies back then. But I still love the Grinch. *You're a mean one, Mr. Grinch….*" He sang in a deep rumble, not half bad, and she giggled, totally charmed. Nothing in the world was as much fun as the silly intimacy following a good night of sex. Only this felt more intimate than usual, certainly more unexpected. And the sex had been *really* good.

"Is your mom still alive?"

"No."

The syllable was abrupt, but she felt pain behind it, not censure, and couldn't help rubbing her cheek against his shoulder, even though he hadn't asked for her sympathy. "I'm sorry."

"Me, too. So what are you asking Santa for this year, Jane?"

"Oh, not much." She smiled in the darkness. "Less stress and hatred among people and nations, more appreciation for the simple and natural and less glorification of crap throughout the world."

"Wow. That's a sackful. No diamonds? Furs? Expensive cars?"

"God, no." She laughed. "Christmas should be about love. Though a clean apartment would be nice. How about you—what do you want?"

"I'm not big into gifts either. Especially since my close family is gone." He spoke lightly and ruffled her hair. "Right now all I want is for this night to go on a lot longer than it can."

Her smile died, replaced by a swell of sadness much deeper than the situation warranted. What kind of sexually free woman was she to be dreading the end while they were still in the middle? She knew it was coming. What more could you expect from an anonymous fantasy come true in the dark? Asking for a name, address or phone number would shatter the perfection of this night.

She lifted her head as if she could see him to speak to. "Do you do this a lot?"

He snorted. "What, go to abandoned inns, get the wrong key and find hot women lying in bed willing to sleep with me?"

"*Dying* to sleep with you. Yes." She smiled, loving that he was funny as well as sexually talented. "That."

"Do I have sex with strangers often—is that what you meant?"

"Yes."

"No. Most of the women I meet these days I work with, and sleeping with coworkers is a very poor idea. I'm not into the bar scene either. You?"

She couldn't help the rush of relief. "No."

A kiss landed on her collarbone, though who knew where he'd been aiming. Did he feel relief, too? "So what made you decide to have it with me?"

"I don't know." She nestled back more comfortably against him. "You sounded sexy and you smelled sexy and you felt sexy, and if you promise not to think I'm kinky…"

"Why wouldn't I want to think you're kinky?"

She giggled. "Good point."

"Tell me."

"Sex with a complete stranger has always been a fantasy of mine. Not someone you meet and talk to all evening and eventually go home with. But someone you meet and go for it right there without knowing anything about each other or bothering to find out."

"Not even a name?"

"No, John Smith, not even that."

"Have you tried to do it before?"

"God, no." She tucked his arm back firmly around her. "It's ridiculously dangerous. I might be kinky, but I'm not an idiot."

"That's good to know. Why do you think that kind of sex appeals to you?"

"Hmm." She thought it over, wondering why she was

talking so easily with him about something she'd only had the nerve to tell her own sister the day before. "Maybe I knew subconsciously how good the sex would be?"

"You think the sex between us is good only because of the dark?"

"I...don't know. Could be. What do you think?"

"I doubt it's only that."

She swallowed so loud she was sure he'd heard it. *Will we ever find out?* "Maybe not."

"Can I offer advice I'm in no position to be giving?"

"Sure."

"I wouldn't make a habit of this sex-with-strangers thing."

"No? Why not?" As if she didn't know....

He started stroking her hair, long, soft, gentle strokes that made her want to purr now and find room for him in her suitcase later. "Because I don't want to worry about you being found hacked to pieces."

She shivered, half in revulsion, half in gooey enjoyment of his protectiveness. "I guess I'll count myself lucky to have found you and leave it at that."

"Sounds much safer. And I'm feeling pretty lucky, too, Jane Doe."

She beamed, touched her nose to his warm, slightly prickly jaw, then yawned in spite of herself, overcome by delicious, postsexual fatigue. She listened to his breathing gradually slowing, wondering how her real name would sound in that thrilling deep voice, feeling sleepy but unwilling to sleep yet. Instinctively she knew dawn would come too soon, and with it the end of the fantasy. She'd see him then. Wouldn't she? Would the sight of each other take them closer to knowing each other or father away?

"Do you live in Maine?"

His answer was a sleepy grunt in the negative. No other information offered. No questions asked in return. Message received: No fishing or hunting for identifying details allowed without a permit.

She should have expected the tiny stab of disappointment. But how was she ever going to go back to her ordinary life after an adventure this spectacular? Back to the endless run of male disappointments. She wanted to bottle the magic of tonight and stow it in her travel bag for all those lonely nights ahead when she'd think back to how right it felt to be with him. How comfortable…

She knew better but couldn't help the wistful feeling that if either of them were willing to risk it, they might be more to each other than one-time lovers.

Maybe in the morning she'd try again….

When she woke it was light. And John Smith, her perfect fantasy lover…was gone.

6

"OH MY GOD, LUCY, it was so amazing. It was so *amazing*."

"Wow." Lucy cringed hearing her own voice come out so low and tight. But she couldn't help it. She knew she was supposed to be happy for her sister, happy that Krista got herself massively laid by a stranger she'd never even seen in daylight, but sorry, she was just pissed. *Pissed!*

"You don't sound amazed."

"I'm amazed. Trust me." She picked up the file her boss had asked for and rapped it sharply on her desk. The stupidity. The sheer *stupidity*. Even as well as she knew her sister's appetite for diving in without checking for sharks, she couldn't help being appalled at this behavior. Sex! With someone she hadn't even *seen*. Krista should be thanking her lucky stars she was *alive*, not bragging about every pant and heave.

"Okay, I'm sensing a serious dose of sisterly disapproval here, Lucy. Just let me have it, okay?"

"Krista." She bit her lip. Yelling at people was not her strong suit. "He could have killed you. He still could. He could have followed you home and—"

"It wasn't like that."

Lucy rolled her eyes and slapped the file back on her desk so hard half its contents spilled out. Right. It was magic. It was fireworks. It was Orgasms "R" Us. Like the last guy and the one before that and the one before that. Though at least Krista got a glimpse of previous men before she slept with them. When was she going to get a clue that relationships were not all fun and excitement and games and adrenaline rushes? "How do you know it was safe? You couldn't even *see* him. You couldn't look into his eyes and see if he was decent or honest or—"

"I didn't need to."

"This from the woman who writes Get Real? Get real, Krista." She took the phone away from her left ear. Took a breath and put it back to her right. She was shaking. She was so damn furious she was shaking.

"Jeez, Lucy, I've never heard you like this." Her sister's voice quieted. "I'm really worried about you."

"You're worried about *me?*" She turned her chair toward her computer and bent forward so she couldn't be overheard by anyone walking past. "You're off screwing strangers blind and *I'm* the one who needs help?"

"I know it sounds nuts. Believe me, I do. But you weren't there. You didn't hear him talking. He was a normal, nice, funny, fabulous guy who—"

"Thought nothing of putting the moves on a woman who could be the next Aileen Wuornos. Clearly he's never seen *Monster.* Or *Fatal Attraction.* What was he thinking? What were you both thinking? Weirdos are out there. Stuff happens. Bad stuff. You have to act responsibly or—"

"Okay. Look. I'm sorry. You're right. It was crazy. But you're also implying that I have no common sense and couldn't tell a complete lunatic from a guy who got the wrong key by mistake."

"And how much experience with lunatics have you had so you're so sure you'd recognize one?"

Her boss's door opened abruptly. "Lucy?"

Lucy jerked upright and whirled guiltily in her chair. "Yes, Alexis. Sorry. Here's the Johnson file, I'll be off the phone in a second." She swept the file's contents back into the folder and stood to hand it over apologetically.

"No problem." Alexis smiled in that way that told Lucy it was a problem and returned to her office.

"I gotta go, Krista."

"Okay, truce?"

"Truce. We can talk later." Lucy hung up the phone, still seething. Damn it. She was sitting there at her perfect desk in her boring, sensible job with a boss who got antsy over one personal call, unable to care enough to move her performing career to the next level, in love with a wonderful man she was losing and fascinated by a sexy one she couldn't let herself touch.

As if that wasn't bad enough, she'd been blessed with an older sister to compare herself to who threw herself haphazardly through life, making risky, inappropriate choices and everything magically worked out. What was it, *one day* after she'd confessed her fantasy of sex with a stranger, the damn thing came true? Who made those odds? Who ordered her world so that everything always fell into place, while Lucy couldn't make one thing come out right, not her love life, not her—

"Hey, there."

She started, adrenaline rushing like Niagara Falls. "Hi, Josh."

"You surviving?" He sauntered around her desk and

winked one of his big, dark-lashed Orlando Bloom eyes. "Big boss woman in a mood today, huh."

"Shhhh." She cautioned him at the same time her eyes flicked to her phone and saw Alexis was on a call.

"Is she being rough on you?"

"No rougher on me than the rest of my life." She tried to laugh, to make the tense statement into a big joke, but the laughter fell flat, too.

"Uh-oh." He touched her, that gentle two-fingered prod to the shoulder, but she felt the quivers all the way down to her...never mind. "I think you need a drink today, Lucy. Even a small one would help."

She swallowed hard. Thought of Link. Of how she hadn't slept again last night, of his increasing exasperation with her misery. Of the breakdown of their communication, the cessation of their sex life. Of how he'd turned down her invitation to have lunch today. Granted, her office was downtown by Faneuil Hall and his was in Cambridge, but he'd risen high enough in his architectural firm to take more than an hour for lunch if he wanted to.

If he wanted to.

"How about this?" He touched her arm again, leaned forward until she caught a whiff of his cologne. Sexy, spicy, dangerously attractive like the rest of him. "You can sit at a separate table, I'll buy you a cocktail and watch you drink it."

That started her laughing—until for a horrible second she was afraid she'd switch and start crying instead. How bad of an idea was it to go out for a drink with this man?

How much worse would it be to go home to more strained silence and forced conversation and memories of a wonderful, passionate past she couldn't figure out how to turn back into their future?

She thought of Krista, taking on life's opportunities without second thoughts or third ones or fourth ones....

She'd go. God forgive her. She'd go. Maybe Josh was a sign. Maybe he'd been sent either to panic her into saving her relationship or show her it was time to move on. She needed to find out.

"Okay." She tried to smile up at him, but after a glimpse into those eyes, the guilt forced her gaze down to her desk. Only it bounced right back up again. "One drink. A platonic drink with a colleague."

"Absolutely." He grinned triumphantly. "My hands will stay in my own lap the whole time. Er, I mean…"

Lucy giggled; he smiled and winked. A horrible weight lifted from her shoulders…and sank, ker-splash, into the pit of her stomach. She could call this a platonic drink until she was blue in the face, but she was attracted to Josh as she hadn't been attracted to any man since she'd first set eyes on Link, red-faced, sweating, radiating masculine heat, returning from an early morning jog as she was on her way to an eight o'clock sociology class, carefully dressed and made-up for her day. This one platonic drink was as close to unfaithful as she'd ever been. As close as she was ever going to get.

She made it through the last hour of work, leaving a choked, forced message for Link that she'd be home late. That she was having a drink after work with a colleague. When she got home she'd tell him who. No point making him sit there miserably thinking the worst when the worst wasn't even going to come close to happening.

She ignored the tiny needling voice that told her she'd

been a fixture in Link's life so long he probably wouldn't even think to get jealous. Which should have relieved her but depressed her even more.

He took her for granted.

The second she had the thought, panic bloomed. No, he didn't. No way. They were meant to be together. She just needed to find a way to make it work.

She should cancel this drink. She was a fool thinking she could find happiness anywhere but where she belonged. With—

"Ready?"

She turned at the sound of Josh's voice, took in the eager glint in his sexy eyes. Link had looked at her that way once and for years after. He'd looked at her that way even the very first time, when he'd stopped her on her way to class and introduced himself. And she'd been so damn sure he always would.

"Yes." She stood and grabbed her purse, put her pen away in the holder on her desk. "I'm ready."

They walked together through the offices of Stenkel, Webb and Reese, Josh calling out good-nights to people he knew, which appeared to be everyone. She was flattered he seemed anxious to call attention to them, but frankly she would much rather put on dark glasses, a hat and a trench coat and sneak out on her hands and knees.

Worse, instead of taking her to one of the bars around Faneuil Hall, where most of the employees of Stenkel, Webb and Reese hung out, where the buzz and press of humanity was comfortingly nonintimate and slightly deafening, he took her in a cab to the Oak Bar at the Copley Plaza Hotel, an elegant place of wood, mirrors, marble and gilt, upholstered chairs and dark wood tables with candles. He even ordered her a glass of champagne, her favorite, remembering some comment she'd made to him weeks ago, when his interest had started becoming apparent.

A beautiful place. A handsome man. Champagne. Enough to get a girl a bit dizzy. Why didn't she and Link ever come to places like this? It wasn't as if they couldn't afford it. And if Link was too tired to come out, why didn't she ever buy champagne and bring it home?

Because champagne was for joy and celebration, and she hadn't had a lot of reasons for either lately.

Josh grinned and lifted his martini to her as if she was the most precious thing in his life, and they drank the first sip together, which felt intimate and thrilling and awkwardly wrong all at the same time.

"So…" He dragged his chair around to the side of the table next to her. "Tell me about Lucy. Something I don't know and wouldn't suspect."

"Oh, well…" She resisted the urge to shift her own chair away. His knee was inches from hers. "Let's see. I'm not that exciting really."

He snorted in disagreement. "I'll be the judge of that."

She sipped her champagne again, loving the elegant tickle of bubbles in the smooth wine taste, loving that he seemed to think she was so fascinating. "Obviously you know about my job. I have an older sister who is a writer and who lives—"

"Lucy." He interrupted gently. "I didn't ask about your sister."

"Oh. Right." She laughed, feeling stupid, and drank more champagne, suddenly not caring that she was probably emptying the glass too quickly. "I grew up in Framingham. My mom is a kindergarten teacher, my dad runs a print shop. I got good grades, always behaved well, never—"

"Always?" He lifted both eyebrows, mischievous, challenging.

"Yeah." She sighed. "Boring, huh."

"You never got into trouble?"

"Not really." She wanted to say she was pretty sure she was getting into trouble right then and there, but that might sound as though she was inviting something and she didn't want that. So she told him a few silly stories of pranks she and Krista had pulled—the usual kid stuff, ringing doorbells, goofy phone calls—jokes Krista loved, which had made Lucy anxious and guilty.

The way she felt when Josh ordered her more champagne without asking if she'd like another.

"Are you trying to get me drunk?"

"No." He shook his head and grinned his bedroom grin. "I'm trying to get you loose and happy so you can have some fun. I get the feeling you don't have enough."

"Oh." She frowned down at her fingers twisting in her lap, trying to quell the warmth over his concern for her. "Maybe not. My sister has all the fun. She just called and told me she—"

He waited, then touched her fingers, squeezed her hand and let go. "She what?"

Lucy drained her champagne. This was mined territory. "Nothing. I'm sorry. I'm not used to drinking."

"It's okay. You don't have to tell me anything you don't want to." His voice was low, soft, gentle, his eyes deep and soulful as a puppy's. She loved puppies—and nearly giggled at the thought. Damn her low tolerance for alcohol. "Tell me something else about you, Lucy."

She stared at the second glass the waiter had set in front of her. Stared, then picked it up and took a sip. She could guess what would happen if she told him about the singing and the dancing and the acting. A lot of people were excited by that kind of creativity. They equated it to near stardom or something equally crazy.

But what the hell. "You probably don't know that I'm a singer. And an equity actress. I sing at Eddie's Lounge every other Tuesday night."

"Wow." He gazed at her rapturously and she had to look down before she got too giddy. "That's incredible. Why the hell did you say you were dull?"

"I don't know…I've been doing it so long, it doesn't feel so…well, I don't know why I said that."

Why the hell *had* she said that? Since when had her self-esteem dropped that low?

She didn't want to start thinking about Link again….

"You're incredible, Lucy. I'd like to come hear you."

"Oh. Wow. Thank you." His praise made her want to get up and sing right there. But the thought of him in the audience at Eddie's made her uncomfortable. To perform for strangers was one thing. Link had long stopped coming, not that she blamed him, she guessed. But to perform with someone like Josh in the house…

"Are you performing tomorrow night?"

"Next week."

He clinked his glass to hers. "I'll be there, babe. Unless you want to go karaoke after this so I can hear you tonight."

She was shaking her head before he finished speaking. "I can't go anywhere after this."

"Why not?"

"Because it's not a good idea."

"It's a great idea. Why do you say that?"

"I need to get home." She gripped her glass too hard and had to remind herself to ease up.

His eyes narrowed quizzically. He leaned forward, which made her want to lean forward, too, and also lean as far away as she could get. "Lucy, I want to be your friend. I think I've made that pretty clear. And friends can talk to each other. I want to tell you there is something really creepy about the way you've isolated yourself from life for this guy."

She nearly spit out a mouthful of champagne. "What?"

"Look, don't get me wrong. I don't know Luke at—"

"Link."

"Link, sorry. I don't know Link at all. But I'm getting to know you. And I sense that you're a passionate, exciting, dynamic woman."

Her heart gave a little jump on each word, starting with *passionate* and ending with *woman*. Oh my lord, she so wanted to be all those things to someone again.

"Thank you," she whispered. What the hell else could she say when the only thing going through her alcohol impaired consciousness was *Kiss me now and don't stop?*

"But you're acting like a timid fifties housewife whose goal in life is to heat Link's meat loaf for him every night so he won't starve to death."

Lucy's mouth dropped open. The champagne swimming invitingly through her veins stopped and tread water. "I do not."

He winked. "Do, too."

She gulped more champagne and laughed so she wouldn't get angry—or pay too much attention to what he'd just said or to the fear starting to weigh down her chest.

"Lucy, a man shouldn't drag you down. He should lift you up. Make you feel like you can do anything, be anything."

He covered her hand with his, gazing earnestly, and she didn't pull it away even though she knew she should.

"A man should make you feel that through it all he'll be right there beside you, supporting you." His voice dropped, became husky and hesitant. "Loving you."

Her eyes met his and this time she couldn't look away. Her head became buzzy and delicious again, and she didn't think she could entirely blame the alcohol.

This was completely insane. Worse than she ever imagined. How could she be so stupid as to think it was a good idea to come out with him? What did she imagine it would solve? She'd been crazy to listen to Krista or compare herself at all to her sister. This date was just making a complicated situation much, much more complicated.

"I need to go." She got up and fumbled with her purse. "How much is the—"

"No, no, don't go. I'm sorry." He stood and grabbed her arm, pulled her gently until she was much too close and minded much too little. "Please don't go. I didn't mean to scare you off. I'm just—I hate to see you unhappy."

Lucy swallowed, feeling her face flush hot. She wasn't unhappy. She wasn't. She was just in a little teeny rut right now.

She opened her mouth to speak, changed her mind, opened it again, changed her mind again…and noticed him watching her lips in a very intent way.

And then—oh my God—she knew. He was going to try to kiss her. And if she didn't put a stop to it now, right now, immediately, pronto, ASAP, then it was going to be too…

His lips touched hers once, then again, and a swath of fire roared down her body, heart to her toes and back up.

Oh no.

Way, way too late.

HIS CELL PHONE WAS ringing. Again.

Seth grabbed a Post-it and stuck it halfway down the page in the file where he'd left off reading. A terminated employee was suing Wellington Department Stores for age discrimination. As far as Seth could tell, she was fired for not showing up to work and not working when she showed up. But no doubt if she got hold of the media or they got hold of her, the story would emerge quite differently.

He hauled out his cell and rolled his eyes at the display.

"Hi, Aimee. I'm in the middle of three thousand things. What's up?"

"You're always in the middle of three thousand things."

Except when he'd been in the middle of the Maine woods and only one passionate, thrilling thing. "Yeah, well, that's adulthood."

"I want to tell you something really cool."

He slumped onto his elbow on the desk. Her idea of cool and his rarely intersected. They were fifteen years apart, but he felt like her grandfather sometimes. At his board meeting the day he left for Maine, he'd barely managed to keep the members' enthusiasm going for the reopening in spite of the excellent presentation by his head buyer. Everything rested on Aimee and the new ad campaign. Whatever "cool" thing his stepsister had to tell him better not mean trouble. "Okay, I'm listening."

"I'm gonna write a novel!" Her normally high voice squeaked higher with excitement. "Isn't that great?"

"A novel." He could barely stand to think about it.

"Yeah! Juice says I'm a natural writer."

"He does." Seth sat up and then leaned back, let his head drop, staring at the white ceiling of what he still thought of as his father's office, one he'd been allowed in only a few times, even after he'd joined the company at the retail level in his teens. Juice says? The man couldn't even find his way to Skowhegan. "And what kind of expert on writing is Juice?"

"You didn't know?"

Seth sighed. "Tell me."

"Juice writes poetry. And short stories."

Oh, Seth would just bet. Ode to an Overflowing Bra Cup.

"He's had a bunch published, one in *The New Yorker*.

That got Seth's head vertical. "You're kidding."

"Well, not really, I mean, he almost got it in. But he has published in magazines. Maybe a couple. I don't know their names. Anyway, I was talking to him about this idea for a book about this girl who becomes a superstar at, like, age nineteen, and this crazed fan starts harassing her, so she hires a bodyguard and they fall in—"

"Aimee."

"Yeah?"

"People struggle years and years learning to write before they—"

"Oh, I know, but Juice already has me with an agent and she thinks they can get me a high-six-figure advance by the middle of the month. The book will probably go to auction."

Seth closed his eyes. When this got out, Krista Marlow was going to have no mercy. And neither was his board. It was entirely possible Aimee was the next Faulkner, but he'd bet his drawers she could write only as well as she could act, sing and dance.

As far as he was concerned, her only brilliant talent was for personal drama.

He needed to sit down and talk to her. He needed to be a stronger father figure or something. But damn it, for one thing he was not her father. For another, he had an already heavily loaded plate, his own life to live. And for a third...

He hated getting involved in female hysteria.

"Are you going to have time to write a novel and act in a show and be the spokesperson for Wellington Department Stores?"

"Oh, jeez, I did the dumb commercials. How much more is there?"

"Aimee." He picked up a pencil and braced it between his thumbs. "The board approved budget for a trial year of appearances and possibly more commercials next year. If this hits, you're going to be at it a long time."

She gave a childish whimper. "I don't want to."

"It's your family, Aimee." His attempt at patience wasn't working very well. "In terms you'd understand, it's about the money that makes your lifestyle possible. This is only giving back a little."

"A little too much."

The pencil snapped. "I gave up a huge part of my life for this company and all I expect of you is—"

"But you like all that boring stuff. It's who you are. I'm different, I'm more creative, more spontaneous, more... alive."

"Right." He sighed. No point. There was just no point. "Well, Mr. Stuffy here still expects you to toe the company line. Until you're twenty-five, your money comes through me."

"Oh, fine, Seth." Her auto-tears mechanism kicked in, complete with oh-so-adorable sniffles. "Threaten your own sister. Real nice. Maybe you could just try a little harder to screw up my life, okay?"

"Good plan. I'll get right on it."

The line went dead.

And another scintillating conversation with his bratty stepsister was over.

He went back to the file and removed the Post-it, trying to get his brain to calm down enough to read the words. Exactly how creative, spontaneous and alive was he ever allowed to be?

One recent time, last Friday to be precise, immediately refilled his imagination. With Krista. In the darkness of the cabin. He had felt alive then in a way that still managed to startle him awake at night, hard as iron.

Coming back to…this—he closed the file, glanced with disgust around the dark cherrywood old-boy office—had been agony. Like returning to an iron lung when you'd been given time to get out and breathe on your effortless own.

But Krista couldn't happen again. How many times could he be a faceless stranger in the dark? Only once. And if Krista found out he was Aimee's stepbrother, what they had would come crashing down from the weightless freedom of anonymity into the high-gravity prison of a relationship.

Or assault and battery.

That kind of perfection shouldn't be repeated—couldn't be repeated. No point in giving it another thought.

Never mind that way too many of his waking minutes were spent hungry for her again.

A knock at his door. He glanced at his watch. Nearly seven. He needed to get something to eat. "Come in."

"Hello, there." Mary. Wearing a Santa hat she managed to make look sexy, a short-skirted suit that showed off her long legs and a plunging blouse displaying more cleavage than daytime required. Not that he was complaining.

"All work and no play, Seth. I was passing by your building on my way home, hoped to entice you into having something to eat." She sat on the edge of his desk and laid a neatly wrapped package in front of him. "Merry Christmas."

"Mary." He chuckled, while his brain made a mental note to ask Sheila to hunt some token up for Mary, too. "You shouldn't have—"

"Oh, I know. I wasn't planning to get you anything. But I saw this and couldn't resist. Open it."

He put on a smile, hating having to open presents in front of the giver when his reaction would be on display. The ribbon untied easily, the wrapping slid off....

A cartoon in a frame. Executives in suits, red-faced, sweating, running frantically around a circular track. On the sidelines, rats in lounge chairs, in sunglasses, holding drinks. The caption: *Who's racing?*

Seth forced a chuckle. "This is fabulous."

"Isn't it?" She laughed and swung her legs so her skirt moved higher. "I knew you'd love it."

"I do love it." He hated it. Why the hell would he want a reminder that he was trapped on the track? In a bizarre jump of logic, his brain told him Krista wouldn't have given him anything like this.

He held the print up and made himself laugh again.

This time the bitterness probably showed. What the hell was he doing fantasizing about Krista and exchanging gifts? "Thanks, Mary, this was very sweet of you."

"Don't mention it." She leaned forward. "So are you hungry at all?"

His eyes dropped. So shoot him, he was a man and she was stunning. "Starving."

"For food?"

Hmm.

He pushed the stubbornly clinging thoughts of Krista away. Maybe a night with Mary was what he needed. She was passionate, exciting and most of all loyal and discreet, never mixing business into their pleasure, never expecting special treatment or favors on the board because of their on-and-off liaison. Nor did she ever expect their relationship to stay exclusive or stray out of the bedroom. His ideal woman.

Or so he'd always thought.

He stood and leaned on the desk so their faces were closer than business decorum dictated, watched her eyes widen and go dark, her lips part. He let his gaze linger again on her cleavage, remembering the bounce and firm feel of her breasts in his hands, trying to conjure up as many arousing images of their sexual gymnastics as he could.

Still trying.

Trying again.

Damn.

He felt nothing but a desire to find some way, any way, using whatever possible imagination or means at his disposal, to get Krista Marlow in bed with him again.

IMAGINE YOURSELF stressed, strained, wrung out. The work week has been hell. Your significant other barely glances your way. No energy to cook. House needs cleaning, decorating. Presents to buy for too many people. Same old drunks at the same old office parties. Sound familiar?

Now imagine you and your SO leaving the office Friday, maybe an hour or so early, driving into the peace and pine-tree serenity of the Maine woods. No decorations but the ones nature put there. Not a soul around...

Except for the sexiest body and voice in the darkness you could ever even hope to fantasize about.

Your cabin waits, cozy, warm, fireplace flickering.

Assuming the damn thing works.

Silence so comforting and beautiful you can hear your own thoughts. Only the call of birds or breezes singing through needled boughs...

Or the scream of the wild orgasm.

Krista sighed and pushed her laptop off her lap, grabbed a handful of Nature's Way organic tortilla chips from the bag she'd plopped onto her still-unmade bed and started crunching. Damn it. The article was stupid and boring, and writing about the trip was hell.

She wanted him back. The glow of the experience last weekend had lasted the rest of her trip, all the way home and all this week.

Then, thud, it had given way to the reality of her life. Without him. Without anything but work and friends and family and…well, okay, she was damn lucky, those were all pretty incredible.

But not magical. Not light-me-up fabulous. Not writhe-in-ecstasy supreme.

Call her greedy, but having her fantasy satisfied hadn't satisfied her. It had only kindled her appetite. Not for more sex with more strangers. No way. Talk about an unhealthy, disaster-inviting lifestyle.

But for more sex with him. With John Smith or whatever his name actually was. There were other men she'd enjoyed only once, though she never entered into a one-night stand intending it to be just that. Either the guys decided once was enough, *hasta la vista* baby, and thanks, whoosh, gone. Or she turned off, though that was much rarer—if she made it as far as the bedroom, chances were she liked them enough to keep trying. Or neither ever made the effort to see the other again and the whole thing quietly died off. She'd been disappointed some, cried a bunch of times, gotten cranky way more often than that.

Nothing like this. She was obsessed, flattened, miserable. A few hours in contact with someone she knew nothing about and her world had been rocked as hard as her body.

What the hell was that?

She scooted off the bed and marched into her kitchen to root for a jar of salsa in the refrigerator. Was she so shallow that the only guy she'd ever been this excited about was one she knew next to nothing about? Or had there been an extraordinary connection that meant something?

Why couldn't fate have given her the chance to find out?

Salsa in one hand, bottle of natural-flavored water in the other, she closed the squeaky refrigerator door with her foot and made her way back to the bed. She wasn't a control freak. High-strung, yeah, okay, but she took things in stride most of the time or found ways around any obstacles.

She settled back on the bed, twisted open the salsa, dunked a chip and gave her laptop a disparaging glare for still being there, reminding her of work that still needed doing. She wanted John Smith again—and again and again and again—and all her energy was wasted slamming over and over into the brick wall there was absolutely no way to avoid. The very fact that made the fantasy so exciting and arousing and intriguing also made it doomed never to be repeated.

John Smith was a stranger. He'd disappeared sometime during the night, not to cabin nine, but to wherever he'd driven. She'd been pathetic enough to linger at the Pine Tree Inn a couple of hours after it was time to move on to her next destination, hoping maybe he'd run out for breakfast for the two of them, maybe had a flat, maybe gotten lost....

Yeah. Her maybes never worked with men. She could publish a four-hundred-page volume of all the rational reasons men might have disappeared, and it always came down to *because they wanted to be gone.*

John Smith wanted to be gone. And Krista was still having a terrible time accepting it.

She poured salsa off the edge of a chip into her mouth and crunched the chip viciously. Yes, folks, you heard it here. Krista Marlow, author of Get Real, was having trouble getting exactly that.

Her phone rang and set off a charge of adrenaline. The latest one. Her adrenal gland was working so much overtime these days she expected a strike notice any day. Talk about needing to get real. John Smith didn't even know her real name, let alone her phone number.

She stood, brushing tortilla chip crumbs off her black top, and picked up the call. "Hello?"

"Hey, there." The voice was deep, masculine...familiar, but not the right one. She knew because her adrenal gland yawned and went back to sleep.

"Hey, there what?" Who the heck was this? She started pacing. For some unknown reason she was unable to hold still during a phone conversation.

"It's Sam."

"Sam!" Right, of course. Sam. Ex-boyfriend who reappeared periodically and he and she, um, sorta took up where they left off for a while and then stopped again. Nice, comfortable itch scratch when she needed one.

"Ho ho ho, little girl, have you been good this year?"

"I'm always good, you know that." Hmm. An itch scratch sounded like a really good idea to brighten up her December, take her through the holidays in a more cheerful manner. "Great to hear from you, Sam. How's it going?"

"Fine. I was thinking about you this morning, wondering what you were up to."

Translation: My latest girlfriend and I broke up a while ago.

"Oh, that's nice. Well, the writing is going well, I'm keeping busy...."

"Anyone in your life right now?"

Translation: Are you already getting some?

Krista smiled. Pictured Sam as she'd last seen him— tall, blond, nice build, neat goatee. Cute, energetic, funny, good time in the bed and out.

Just what she needed.

An image came to her—okay, no, it had been totally dark, so it wasn't an image. A memory then. Powerful arms around her; her body joined to his, straining to join harder; the feel of his lips on her skin; the sound of his voice...and the intensity of the physical connection that somehow, no matter how impossible it seemed, had spilled over into the emotional. At least for her.

Anyone in your life right now?

Not anyone real.

"Hello, Earth to Krista."

Sam's voice jolted her out of her lustful daydream and she shook her head. "Sorry, I'm here. Sorry."

"I asked if you were seeing someone. Sounded like you were having a hard time deciding."

She opened her mouth to say the words, *There's no one in my life,* but they wouldn't come. The truth? John Smith wasn't in her life. But he sure as hell existed strongly enough in her head right now that she was shocked to find she had no room for Sam.

How self-destructive was that?

"There...is someone in my life right now."

"Bummer. Is he worthy of your perfection?"

"Oh...yes." Her throat threatened to close up. Tears stung. What the hell was the matter with her? She should be laughing and teasing Sam right back.

"Wow. Sounds serious."

"I guess." She closed her eyes. Serious Krista-the-Nutcase, more like it.

"Okay. Well, I wish you all good things, Krista. Merry Christmas, happy new year and all that."

"Thanks, Sam. To you, too. I'll see you around." She said goodbye and punched off the phone, slumped down onto her gray-and-white-striped couch, near the black ink stain that looked like a rat.

Oh my lord. She needed her head examined. She'd just turned down good sex with a really nice man for the memory of one night of unrepeatable perfect sex with...who knew?

Her incoming e-mail notifier started in—loud footsteps of a cartoon butler who walked somberly onto the screen and announced in an upper-crust British accent that she had mail.

Probably spam. She sighed and went to check.

No. Not spam.

A message from the Pine Tree Inn owner, Betty Robinson. That alone was enough to get her heart pounding. Anything containing the words *pine tree* would probably make her feel alternately jazzed and wistful for the rest of her life. She'd make sure to get a Frazier fir when she went tree shopping.

Ms. Marlow,

We hope you enjoyed your stay. The following e-mail was sent to our office; the gentleman requested we forward it to you. Hope you are well and that we'll see you again next time your travel brings you to Maine.

Sincerely,

Betty and Arnold Robinson

Oh.

Oh, my.

Oh, oh, *oh, my.*

Forget pounding. Her heart was slam-dancing. Quick, before she opened it, who else could it be from, before she assumed it was John Smith and then got bitterly disappointed when it wasn't. No one she knew would have reason to e-mail her anywhere but her home account...

Light-headed and shaky, trying to calm herself down and failing miserably, she opened the attachment. Another e-mail.

Dear Jane Doe,
I didn't get enough of you. Could I ever?
I'd like to find out.
Ritz-Carlton Hotel, room 329, Monday, December 12, 7:00 p.m.
John Smith

7

NERVOUS DIDN'T EVEN begin to describe it.

Krista stood just down the silent hall from room 329 at the Ritz-Carlton, staring at the door, amazed that her feet had agreed to carry her even this far.

Damn Lucy and her cautious nature. Some of her warnings had finally penetrated Krista's delirious haze. She'd barely slept the night before, both from excited anticipation and anxious dread. The middle of the night was the what-if demon's favorite time to strike.

What if...? What if...? What if...?

What if John Smith was a psycho weirdo who liked to toy with his victims several times before executing them?

What if he knew who she was and was stalking her? He might have seen her Massachusetts plates, but his e-mail had just said Ritz-Carlton—he hadn't specified Arlington Street or any other direction or clue an out-of-towner would need to know. How did he know she was from the Boston area?

What if he was married? Why a hotel? She hadn't felt a ring, but that meant nothing.

And her biggest question: with all these doubts and fears, why had she shown up?

Why wasn't she messing up the sheets with big, comfortable, funny Sam, who she wanted so desperately to fall madly in love with and couldn't ever manage to?

What did that say about the Get Real queen that she'd chosen this fantasy instead?

She knew. In her heart she knew. Because it was irresistible. Because whatever had happened between them that night in Maine a week and a half ago, she wanted to know if she could feel it again, this time being able to see him. She wanted to find out if the passion and thrill were simply products of the darkness and the remoteness and the excitement of fear and the surprise of it all or if there was something—dare she use the word?—real between them.

And because even deeper, in her deepest heart of hearts, she believed that if he meant her harm, she would have suspected, that something would have tipped her off, that her instincts would have warned her away.

Yes, he could be married...or he could be protecting himself by choosing a hotel. He knew as little about her as she did about him; it was only sensible not to invite her to his home until they knew each other better. And why bother with a bar or restaurant meeting when a bed was what they really wanted?

Of course, the Ritz was a damn fine touch. No hourly motel in a bad neighborhood for her lover.

She smiled, took a few steps closer to the door. Adrenaline pulled the smile back off her face. Okay, she was terrified anyway. Seeing him in person would put the whole fantasy in—excuse the pun—a different light.

In front of the door now. Deep breath, then she'd count to ten and go in.

One...two...three...

The handle of the door turned. Krista stopped counting. Stopped breathing. Looked up to where she imagined his face was going to appear.

Call her shallow, but she desperately hoped he'd be as attractive to her by sight as he was by touch and personality. Didn't have to be to-die-for handsome but to have that chemical spark visually....

The door swung inward about a foot. Behind it...

Darkness.

So...she wouldn't see him? A stab of disappointment, followed by more questions. Why not? *Was* he married? Anxious she not be able to identify him to the police?

Oh, for heaven's sake, Krista. Hadn't she just been talking about deep-down heart-of-hearts trust?

She stepped forward to the threshold.

"Come in."

His familiar deep voice made her realize retroactively how dreamlike the adventure in Maine had seemed—and how unsure she'd been that it really had happened as she remembered. Hearing him live brought the whole night back to her.

Her nerves switched over into excitement and she took a few steps into the room. More fantasy, more perfect erotic excitement. "John Smith" would stay "John Smith" and she could be his perfect "Jane Doe" for another night.

"Hello, Jane."

She turned and saw his silhouette against the white door, now closed again. Tall and broad, solid and definitely not a dream. An indefinable emotion rose, and she had to relax consciously so it wouldn't escape, though whether it wanted to come out as a giggle or a sob, she couldn't tell.

"Hi." Her voice was breathy and flat.

"I'm glad you're here."

"I am, too."

His dark form stepped toward her, and her already racing heart managed to beat even faster. "I was about to tell you that you look beautiful, but since I can't see you, that's pretty crazy."

Krista laughed unsteadily, understanding him perfectly. If the shape of a man could be beautiful, his was. Certainly to her it was. "I know what you mean. You look... incredible."

He stopped directly in front of her; she could feel the warmth of his body, catch his familiar scent, and the urge to touch was so strong she held back, perversely wanting to stretch the longing to its most unbearable before she gave in.

"I couldn't stop thinking about you."

Krista's breath rushed in, then out. "Me neither."

"I must be losing my mind."

"Mine was gone when I stopped you from leaving the cabin."

"To check your fireplace."

She laughed. "You never did."

"No." He leaned down and rested his forehead against hers. "I had other things I wanted to do for you."

Krista closed her eyes, lips tingling with his nearness. "I remember all of them."

"And I couldn't stop wanting to do them again." His fingertips slid gently along her jawbone, to the back of her head, tipping her face up toward him. "You?"

"Oh, yes."

She barely got the words out before his mouth touched hers and held there, full and warm and still. Then he moved his head slowly, brushing his lips side to side, making her wait for what she wanted.

She was willing to wait. She wanted this night to go on forever. She wanted to feel this erotic charge, this thrill, this mystery, all night long. John Smith and Jane Doe, cloaked in darkness, doing what they did best together.

"Come with me." He found her hand, led her into the room, the furniture ghostly black against dark gray. A huge armoire, a table, the merest hint of light from around heavy curtains.

And a bed.

She followed him toward it, eager to disappear again into the passion.

He stopped next to the bed, drew her to him and kissed her lightly. "Tell me how to undress you."

How? "Top to bottom?"

He chuckled. "I don't know what you're wearing."

"Oh." She smiled, feeling foolish. "Cardigan sweater, only one button done at the waist."

His hands brushed over her stomach, making her fight not to sway toward him. He found the last button and took care of it, pushed the material slowly over her shoulders, left bare by her white linen top. He followed the line of her arms, pressing them behind her to slide the soft knit cotton off her wrists, so her body came flush against his large, warm one and her desire started heating to a serious simmer.

"Done." He murmured the word into her hair, kissed her temple, her cheek, then finally and thrillingly her mouth, a long kiss that made her want him to take over completely.

All in good time. She shouldn't rush what they had all night for.

"What's next?" He spoke against her mouth, trailed his tongue lightly around her lips and kissed her again.

"Buttons…" The simmer was threatening full boil too quickly. "Down my front."

He searched for them, hands brushing across her stomach and breasts. Krista bit her lip to keep from moaning. What had she said about all in good time? This slow pace was going to kill her.

The last button came undone, her top slid off. She stood in her bra and short skirt waiting impatiently for what came next. His hands landed at her waist, large and strong, his torso a black shape looming above her.

"Front closure or back?"

"Front." *And quickly.*

He moved her forward again. His erection bulged from the front of his pants, and she pressed against it, pleased when his breath caught. She wasn't the only one heating.

"Front closures defeat me."

"Allow me." She undid the catch and let the bra drop to the floor, feeling the cool air in the room brushing her breasts, loving the way their whispered words made the darkness even more private.

His hands moved up her waist, thumbs under her breasts, then stroking across the tips, hardening her nipples further. He bent and took one into his mouth, warm, perfect tongue strokes that set her into a rolling boil, nearly spilling over.

She had never, ever wanted a man inside her with the speed and intensity she wanted this one. Was it the darkness? Or was it the man?

He moved his talented mouth to her other breast, covering the first with his hand, keeping the air from chilling her skin, fingering her nipple.

"What's next, Jane Doe?"

"John." Her voice came out as hoarse and low as his. "You…I don't want to wait."

She barely sensed he'd moved before he was kissing her, fiery, openmouthed kisses that disoriented and dazed her. His hands stroked over her breasts again and again, he pushed one leg in between hers.

She moaned, rubbed herself shamelessly against him over and over, yanking up her skirt to rub closer, through the thin lace of her panties. She was crazy, animal, humping this muscular, sexual stranger in the dark, sucking his tongue in and out of her mouth, getting so close to coming she was nearly screaming with it already. One warm hand left her breast, traveled possessively down her back, over her lifted skirt and under her panties. One finger explored, firm pressure down the center line of her buttocks.

She gave a yelp of pleasure, bucked her hips, pushed across his thigh and let it all go crashing through her, rolling, wave after wave, until her knees buckled and she found herself grabbing at his back, trying to ride him even higher.

He growled something she didn't understand, caught her up and dumped her on the bed. She heard him undoing his pants and knew he wasn't going to want it slow either.

He didn't. His pants went down, briefs followed, condom on. She was pretty sure he was still in his shoes.

He spread her wide, moved her panties aside and pushed inside with a groan of pleasure she echoed.

"Jane." He held still. "I've wanted to be back here all week."

"I've wanted you here, too," she whispered.

He started to ride, hard, and she drew her knees up by her shoulders, welcoming his assault, tugging up his shirt to feel his skin on hers.

"I'm not going to last." He pushed himself up on his forearms, slowed his rhythm for five seconds, then pushed harder again. "Not going to."

"I don't care."

"I wanted to." He spoke through clenched teeth, breath in tatters. "I wanted this to be slow…all night. But you are so…I can't."

"Don't wait." She pushed up against him. "Let go. Do it now."

He lunged forward, joined his mouth to hers, and his body tensed, a deep moan came from his throat. He pushed, released, pushed, then his body gradually relaxed; he broke the long kiss into shorter, increasingly gentle ones, then pressed his cheek to hers and lay still.

She clutched the smooth, hard curves of his shoulders, eyes closed, memorizing the feel and smell and weight of his body, feeling that strange upwelling of emotion again—not happiness, not sadness, something in between, mixed and very confusing.

She'd never experienced such pure, perfect passion before. Not even close.

He lifted his head, lifted his body and pulled out of her. Stood and, she guessed by the thumps and swishes of cloth over skin, took off his shoes and pants. She sure as hell hoped he hadn't been putting them back on.

"Be right back."

His silhouette walked across the floor and into the bathroom. The room was silent and strange without him. She moved into the middle of the bed, not sure if she should put clothes back on, take the rest off, stay on top of the bed, move under the covers....

What was going to happen now?

They'd gone at it so fast and furiously, so soon. In the cabin they'd slept between bouts. But what did you do during waking hours with a faceless fantasy in the dark?

He came back into the room, approached the bed, his footsteps light and even in spite of his size. She tensed, feeling awkward, uncertain. Not a familiar or comfortable feeling. Should she offer to leave?

His weight sagged the mattress to her left. "Hey, where are you?"

"Right here."

He slid next to her and caressed her, stomach, breasts, shoulders, his hands warming her rapidly cooling skin. She touched his waist to find him naked and smiled. What had she been thinking, that he'd toss her out—slam, bam, thank you, ma'am?

"What's this?" He tugged the waistband of her skirt. "Off."

She laughed and pulled off the skirt, tossed it onto the floor. "Better?"

"Yes." His hand traveled downward, tugged on the elastic of her panties. "Excuse me?"

Krista giggled and pulled off her panties, too. "Okay now?"

"Perfect." He swept his hand over her, stopping to circle his palm lightly over her sex. "You cold? Your skin is chilly."

"A little."

"Here." He moved up, pulled down the blankets and crawled under with her, pulled her close and let out a deep sigh. "Nice."

"Yes." She closed her eyes and tried to relax, but the silence felt strained and her mind had started running off with a million journalistic questions she wasn't allowed to ask.

"What is it, Jane Doe?"

"What?" She turned instinctively to see his expression and rolled her eyes. See what?

"You're tense as a board. What is it?"

"No, no, I'm fine." She willed every muscle in her body to relax further. How the hell could he tell?

"You're lying." He found the back of her head and brought her face close to his, kissed her—missing her mouth at first, then finding it—long, lazy kisses that made her wish he'd take up residence in her bedroom and come to her every night after lights-out. "Tell me what's bugging you."

"I'm…" She hadn't a clue where to start, how to begin and even if she knew what was wrong. Whereas in the cabin being with him had felt so complete, now there seemed to be some tiny empty corner that needed filling.

She wanted something, she wanted more of him, but not physically, she wanted…

She wanted to know more about him.

But questions would lead to answers, which would lead to a better understanding of who he was and why he wanted her this way, and that could entirely spoil the magic between them.

And yet…the hopeless, eternally optimistic romantic in her wanted to know more anyway. Maybe it wouldn't spoil the magic but make it stronger.

Why was their chemistry so powerful? Who was he? Why the dark? Why a hotel? Why did he want this kind of relationship? Did he think he'd ever want to see her face? Did he—

"Why am I keeping you in the dark?"

Her mouth dropped open. He read minds as well as he read bodies. "Yes. Only I'm not sure I want to know."

"Why?" He rolled onto his back and edged closer again.

"I'm afraid...that knowing too much will spoil it, will spoil this." She turned onto her side, tangled her top leg with his, stroked the coarse hair on his chest. "I mean...maybe it would."

"It's not very complicated."

"No?" Her hand stilled. Being married was complicated. Wasn't it?

"I'm a guy, everything is simple to us." He put his hand over hers and squeezed. "You ready? A dose of guy philosophy?"

"I guess so."

"Here it is." He cleared his throat. "It worked last time, why break it?"

She burst out laughing, and for some reason all the awkwardness disappeared. "You're not married."

"No, ma'am. Never have been. Are you?"

Her breath rushed out in relief. "No, I'm not, not ever. Girlfriend?"

"Negative. Boyfriend?"

"No way. Age?"

"Thirty-six. You?"

"Thirty-two."

"Okay, well that about wraps up the exchange of non-identifying information."

She laughed again. "I guess it does. Back to sex?"

"Too soon for me, I'm embarrassed to admit." He

kissed her and started stroking her shoulder. "Tell me more. Are you happy?"

"Right now?"

"In your life. Would you consider yourself a happy and fulfilled person?"

"Does anyone? Do you?"

"In a lot of ways, yes. Certainly at the moment I would say happy and fulfilled top the list."

She laughed, and her laugh turned to a silly girlie squeal as he dragged her over his body so she was lying on top of him.

"But in some ways you're not happy?" She laid her head on his chest, loving his arms around her, listening to the thud of his heart, hanging on to every delicious sensation of being protected and adored—even in only a carnal sense.

"Work can be…prisonlike."

"What do you do—oops." She slapped her hand over her mouth.

His low chuckle vibrated through her body. "It's very corporate. Very busy. Very pressured. And until recently, not a single opportunity for amazing sex with passionate women in the dark."

"No way!"

"I'm serious."

"So quit."

He sighed. "It's not that easy."

"You're supporting three ex-wives and seven love children around the globe?"

"Eight, how did you know?"

She smiled and gave his neck a gentle bite. "Tell me more."

"Not much to tell." He squeezed her shoulder, then stroked up and down her upper arm. "I can't leave the job, at least right now."

"What would you do if you could?"

His hand on her arm slowed, stopped. She found herself eager for the answer, hoping he wouldn't gloss over it or joke.

"I did a lot of traveling for a year or so after grad school. It wasn't supposed to be for that long, but I got the bug. I had the money and a car and I just went. Landed places, worked for a while, then moved on."

She listened, imagining him picking his words carefully so as not to reveal too much, enthralled and excited that he even wanted to share this with her.

"I grew up in a strange situation. Not damaging so much as...not usual. I wanted to get out there and find out how most of the world lives."

"Did you?"

"No. I mean not really. You can't really experience other people's lives when you have your own to live. But I saw a lot of interesting places and people."

"Tell me."

His hand moved to her hair; obviously he loved to touch, and of course she ate it up.

"In New Mexico I met a woman who lived in a tiny house outside Santa Fe with a view of mountains and desert. She made batik scarves sold in fancy catalogs. Beautiful scarves. Her house smelled of wax, and there were pieces of silk in various stages of completion all over the walls and counters. She lived alone there. I don't think she had much other income. She could walk outside and pick Red Delicious apples from an abandoned orchard."

He picked up a lock of her hair, tugged it and let it drop. Krista barely dared to breathe. As he spoke, she felt something shift inside her. Something about the poetry of his words, the images he painted...this man was more than a talented erection. "Go on."

"She showed me the catalog that sold her accessories. High-quality glossy pictures, full of all these luxury items for office and home and garden, accessories and gizmos no one could possibly need, and there were her scarves among them. Such a story behind them, that tiny little house, and who would ever stop to think of it or of this woman scratching out her living in the middle of a beautiful desert?"

"No one." By now Krista's heart was pounding. He might as well be dictating her next Get Real article for her. This was where she lived, down to her soul. "Tell me about more people you met."

"Let's see. I met a grandmother who ran a bakery in Geraldine, Montana. She made the best blackberry pie I have ever tasted. Her kids and grandkids were after her to sell the recipe or set up a shop, but she refused. She said the recipe was going to die with her because it was God's gift and she wasn't letting anyone else abuse it or profit from it. I stayed there a week, even though I was headed for Seattle. Probably gained five pounds."

Krista tried to laugh but barely made it. She was loving this. She could lie there on top of his warm, extremely gorgeous body and listen to stories like this all night long. "Where did you stay longest?"

"In Maine. I met a man named Hank, a retired lobsterman and widower, way up north in Washington County, a little town called Harrington. I was on my way to Campobello Island and stopped there for dinner. Met this guy at a bean supper and he offered to put me up. I ended up staying all summer, helping him fix up his house, doing a few jobs he couldn't do anymore. He told me how the town had been starved by a highway bypass. How much lobster fishing had changed since he taught his sons."

"I bet." She drank in the words, still trying to wrap her brain around what she was hearing. Most guys talked with this kind of reverence only about motorcycles or baseball or Angelina Jolie. "Tell me more about him."

"I'm talking too much."

"No, I want to hear it."

"Then it's your turn."

"Okay." She kissed his firm, smooth shoulder. "Go on. Tell me about Hank."

"Well…" He tucked his free hand under his head and she sensed he was gathering memories, trying to form a coherent way to describe them. "He'd seen about zero of the world, but he had this peacefulness about him. He wasn't passive, but it seemed to me he'd mastered Zen without consciously trying or even knowing what it was. Crotchety bastard sometimes, but deep down one of the most contented people I've ever met. He read everything. Knew everything. He probably could have done my job better than I could. He knew people, understood them. I felt like I'd stumbled over a spiritual teacher where I least expected to find one."

"Where would you most expect to find one?"

"Good question."

"Not in your parents or in church?"

"No."

His abrupt tone put up an effective Dead End sign Krista respected. "Are you still in touch with Hank?"

"I tried to contact him a few months ago and found out he'd died."

"I'm sorry." Her heart squeezed when it had no business squeezing.

"It was okay." She felt him shrug. "I'd moved on to another life. He had, too. He was ready."

Krista lay on his chest, moving her hands over his shoulders. The silence between them wasn't awkward anymore. She'd never heard a man talk so passionately and sensitively and openly. Not that she thought men weren't capable, just that somehow she never hooked up with that kind of guy. Maybe Lucy was right that she'd always hunted the wrong type of animal. Or maybe because her father had never got much beyond, "Is your homework done?" and "How about those Red Sox?"

"You miss that life."

"In a lot of ways, yes. It was damn fun. Varied, interesting, challenging and enriching."

"So why go corporate?"

"Duty called." His voice became closed, short, the way it had when she'd asked him about his parents. "So tell me about your work."

"I love what I do."

"Lucky."

"I know. I can work at home, at my own pace. Unfortunately I'm my own boss—and I'm a bitch of one."

"Yeah?" He stirred under her.

"Am I too heavy?"

"No. I just got a totally sexy image of you as a bad blond bitch."

Krista frowned. "How did you know I'm blond?"

"I didn't, Jane Doe, but I guess I do now."

"I guess." Relief. She couldn't bear for him to be a creepy stalker now. "So that narrows me down to one out of—what—every five, six, seven women?"

"Tiny, blond, sexy as hell, willing to be with a stranger in the dark—I'd say you're quite unique."

"In a good way?"

"Hell, yes."

She laughed, shocked at how the question had come out. *In a good way?* Like a whiny grade-schooler fishing for whether or not he liked her. When it wasn't supposed to matter whether he liked her or not, since this was Relationship In a Void. Two bodies enjoying the hell out of each other.

She was not going to start hoping for anything. She was not going to start pressing him for anything. She was not going to let this turn into another disaster.

Not.

"So you like the image of me as a bad blond bitch?"

"Mmm, yes."

"Maybe a black bra, black spiky boots, black garter and police cap?"

He ran his hands down to cup her buttocks and push his rapidly firming erection against her. "That'll work."

"Crack my whip, blow my police whistle and order you to pleasure me?"

"Yes, ma'am. How do you want it, ma'am?"

She had to work to keep from giggling. His transformation from smooth operator to cowering submissive was perfect. Only she'd felt the strength in his body and felt it instinctively in his character, so she doubted he was seriously into being dominated. In fact, she had a feeling he wouldn't be able to keep the act going.

"Like this." She pushed herself off him and, straddling him on her knees, moved up until her sex hovered over his mouth. "Pleasure me. Now."

He laughed, low and slightly mischievous, then his tongue started in on her and any thought of being in control of the situation vanished. He was a master, varying the pressure and rhythm until she was a gasping mess, clinging to the head-board, surrendering to the inevitable build toward heaven.

He added his fingers to the mix, pushing inside her with one, then two, making her legs threaten to give way.

He caught her hips and pushed her down to the side. She rolled to her back, spreading wide, eager—no, greedy—for the finish.

His hands grabbed her wrists and held them down by her hips; his forearms rested on her upper thighs, pinning them open. She waited, hearing her own breath, loud and fast in the darkness.

Except he seemed in no hurry to help her out.

"John."

"Mmm?"

"Are you trying to make me lose my mind here?"

"Yessss." She could feel his breath sliding over her sex. He was so close—and so far. "Don't move."

"What?" She lifted her head—stupid since of course she couldn't see him. "Why? What are you doing?"

"Shhh, don't talk." He tightened his hold on her wrists and pushed harder on her thighs, and it suddenly occurred to her he had her completely helpless. "Just listen."

She should be frightened. She should be. He was a complete stranger who had her entirely at his mercy, naked, in a hotel room, and no one else in the world knew where she was.

Any sensible person would be struggling, trying to escape, running to the exit or, even smarter, dialing 911.

She, however, was just getting even more turned on.

Great. Now on top of foolish and reckless she could add twisted.

"Why shouldn't I move?" She listened, wondering if he heard someone coming down the hall or about to knock. "I don't hear anything."

A deep chuckle and more warm breath between her legs that made her squirm and want to lift her hips to his mouth.

"Stay still and listen to your body."

"I know what it's saying." She affected a deep half-crazed voice. "Please make me come. *Now.*"

Another chuckle. "Listen. Relax and listen."

She took a deep breath, forced herself to relax one muscle at a time, toes to knees to stomach to shoulders to scalp, the way her stress-relief tape had taught her. *Clear your mind.* As if *that* ever happened.

"Okay, I'm relaxed."

"Listen." He purred the word. "Just listen."

She made her breathing even and deep, tried to clear her mind and go inside herself the way the meditation portion of her yoga tape instructed her, the way she couldn't ever manage for more than thirty seconds before her brain started chattering at her like a monkey.

Breathe in, out. Breathe in, out. Breathe in, out.

She didn't know how much later—two, five, ten minutes?—something happened. She was alert, aware, and yet…her mind did seem to have reached a quiet place, almost like sleep, and her other senses started taking over. She heard the hum of the heating unit in the room and muffled noises from elsewhere on the floor. She felt the smooth comfort of the quilt underneath her, felt the heat where his forearms and hands touched hers and the slight moisture of their combined skin.

Then the warm weight of his tongue again on her sex. A moan escaped her.

"Shhh. No moving. No noise."

She had to move. She had to. Her hips were straining to rise, her hands wanted to touch him, thread into his hair and go along for the ride.

Somehow she forced herself to lie still, forced her breathing to stay steady and her mind to go back to that calm, clear place.

He pleasured her with painstaking slowness, quick strokes that made her quiver, long slow deep ones that brought her so close, over and over, she thought she'd go completely raving mad.

Except...the peace was bone-deep, the awareness of the sensations so acute, it was almost as if she was climaxing over and over again without climaxing at all. Her awareness of her own body somehow grew and spread to encompass an awareness of his as if they were both inhabiting one body together.

She'd never experienced anything like it.

He stroked her again with his tongue, brought his fingers along to trace her sex in a slow, gentle circle, then closed his lips over her clitoris and sucked with warm, even pressure.

Her orgasm built in slow motion, a low burn that spread and intensified to where she had to fight hard not to gasp, to hold herself still, feeling it gathering force, awed that her body was capable of such power and nearly frightened she'd be carried away somewhere too strange and new.

The peak hit, held and left her gasping silently, wild contractions of pleasure under his fingers.

He kept pace with her, nuzzling her gently, then finally lifted his mouth off her with a kiss that felt reluctant.

"Jane Doe."

"Yes." She could barely even breathe the word out. She was hardly able to form a coherent thought. She'd orgasmed plenty of times with her body, but this somehow involved her mind and her heart in such a powerful combination, she felt raw and vulnerable, as if she'd just lost her virginity to someone vastly more experienced.

"Do you know what happened here?" He loosened her wrist, stroked over her inner thighs.

"I just had the world's best orgasm?" Her voice cracked, making her attempt at humor a joke in itself.

"More than that."

"Two?" She barely did better that time, even with one syllable. This had gone way beyond two bodies in the dark.

"I had you pinned to the bed again, totally submissive." He sounded husky, awed, grateful, humble. "And you not only didn't freak, you gave yourself over to me completely."

He knew. He'd been right there with her and he knew. She felt suddenly so exposed and scared, she wanted to sit up and fumble for her clothes and get the hell out of there as fast as her shaky legs could take her.

Because somehow Krista Marlow, reality queen, despiser of fakery, despoiler of all things glittery and false, had unexpectedly, and quite irrationally fallen halfway in love with a fantasy.

8

"You okay?"

Lucy started at the touch of her accompanist's hand on her shoulder. She'd been sitting at one of the tables in the lounge, staring at a glass of water as if it held the answers she desperately needed. Steve probably thought she'd lost her mind. She wasn't so sure she hadn't.

She and Steve had been performing together on and off since college; he knew her performance routine and moods too well to fool him that this night was like any other. All during her first set she'd been distracted, a little off, trying not to scan the crowd too closely, wondering if Josh were here tonight, though she imagined he'd stick out among the decidedly older crowd that frequented Eddie's Lounge. And as much as she told herself it didn't matter, that he didn't matter, she couldn't help a shameful burn of excitement and hope.

Whether it was hope he'd show or hope he wouldn't, she still hadn't decided. Probably both.

"Thanks, Steve, I'm fine."

He started massaging her shoulders, then reached and waggled her jaw back and forth. "You're tense as a board."

She laughed and pushed his hand away. "I'm fine."

"Link in the audience tonight?"

GET FREE BOOKS and a FREE GIFT WHEN YOU PLAY THE...

Lucky 7

Just scratch off the silver box with a coin. Then check below to see the gifts you get!

SLOT MACHINE GAME!

YES!

I have scratched off the silver box. Please send me the 2 free Harlequin® Blaze™ books and gift for which I qualify. I understand I am under no obligation to purchase any books, as explained on the back of this card.

351 HDL EEXT   **151 HDL EEX5**

FIRST NAME	LAST NAME

ADDRESS

APT.#	CITY

STATE/PROV.	ZIP/POSTAL CODE

7	7	7	Worth **TWO FREE BOOKS** plus a **BONUS Mystery Gift!**
🍒	🍒	🍒	Worth **TWO FREE BOOKS!**
♣	♣	♣	Worth **ONE FREE BOOK!**
🔔	🔔	🔔	**TRY AGAIN!**

www.eHarlequin.com

(H-B-12/05)

DETACH AND MAIL CARD TODAY!

The Harlequin Reader Service® — Here's how it works:

Accepting your 2 free books and gift places you under no obligation to buy anything. You may keep the books and gift and return the shipping statement marked "cancel." If you do not cancel, about a month later we'll send you 6 additional books and bill you just $3.99 each in the U.S., or $4.47 each in Canada, plus 25¢ shipping & handling per book and applicable taxes if any.* That's the complete price and — compared to cover prices of $4.75 each in the U.S. and $5.75 each in Canada — it's quite a bargain! You may cancel at any time, but if you choose to continue, every month we'll send you 6 more books, which you may either purchase at the discount price or return to us and cancel your subscription.

*Terms and prices subject to change without notice. Sales tax applicable in N.Y. Canadian residents will be charged applicable provincial taxes and GST. Credit or debit balances in a customer's account(s) may be offset by any other outstanding balance owed by or to the customer.

BUSINESS REPLY MAIL
FIRST-CLASS MAIL   PERMIT NO. 717-003   BUFFALO, NY

POSTAGE WILL BE PAID BY ADDRESSEE

HARLEQUIN READER SERVICE
3010 WALDEN AVE
PO BOX 1867
BUFFALO NY 14240-9952

NO POSTAGE
NECESSARY
IF MAILED
IN THE
UNITED STATES

"No." The bitterness in her voice surprised her.

Steve pulled out the chair next to her and sat, a burly, balding, comforting presence. "Anything I can do?"

She shook her head and forced a smile. Steve had the healthiest relationship of anyone she knew. He'd met Scott his freshman year at Tufts and that had been it for both of them. So much for the stereotype of the promiscuous gay male.

"Okay, time for round two." Dick, the manager at Eddie's for probably the past two hundred years, swept past them onto the tiny bar stage, picked up the mike and introduced their second set.

Lucy straightened her shoulders, flared her nostrils, consciously following the path of air down through her chest into her lungs, making sure her throat was wide, clear and relaxed.

The audience applauded in its usual enthusiastic fashion. She put on a bright smile, climbed the short set of steps up to the stage and stood beside the piano. This time she was not going to look for him, not going to think about him. She'd relax and get through the second set like she meant it.

"Hey, everyone. We're back. Going to start our next set with a number to make sure you're all in the holiday spirit. Arranged by my fabulous accompanist, Steve Taylor— 'Blue Christmas.'"

She started slow, mournful, bleak, then launched into the great jazzy version that always made her happy, and felt herself starting to relax. If Josh were coming, he would be here by now. She didn't need to get herself all whipped up over nothing. It was a relief, really, that he wasn't.

Except that halfway through the second verse a dark,

slender, graceful man walked in and took a seat at the bar
in the back of the room, gazing around at the cheesy red
and green and gold Yuletide decor with a smirk on his face
she didn't blame him for.

Josh.

She made it through the rest of her song, and the next
one and the one after that—somehow. It was as if the
usual blur of faces she could play to without effort had
shrunk into the background and there was a huge spotlit
version of Josh snagging her vision and attention no matter where she looked or how hard she tried to concentrate
on her singing and the rest of the crowd. She could swear
he didn't take his eyes off her for one second, didn't give
her even that much of a respite. The intensity of that gaze
was making her a little nutty.

"And now, one of my favorites and yours…"

She launched right into the number, tonight keeping the
patter—not her strength anyway—to a minimum. "I've
got you…under my skin."

The crowd applauded briefly at the first familiar
phrase. Josh put down his drink and leaned forward on
his knees, nodding every now and then, as if he'd written the lyrics himself because they had particular reso-
nance for him….

Oh, she was so in trouble.

Worse, she found herself able to look at him a little
more boldly once in a while, found herself playing up the
siren side of the song, found herself wanting to be wildly,
totally, blow-me-away amazing tonight. To prove she
could still be wildly, totally, blow-me-away amazing to
someone. Especially someone like Josh Fairbanks.

The number ended slowly, drawn out. "…under…my

skin." Two beats of silence, then the crowd went wild—except Josh, who didn't applaud, didn't move, sat there staring at her with a smile on his sexy full lips, shaking his head slowly as if he couldn't believe a woman like her even existed.

She bowed to the applause, cheeks burning, and quickly went on to her next song. The rest of the set roared past, song after song, holiday numbers she thought she'd scream if she ever had to sing again felt like old friends at a party where everyone remembers why they all became so close in the first place.

Lucy finished the last note, then the last note of an encore and another—a sultry smoky-bar version of "We Wish You A Merry Christmas"—then sailed off the stage feeling as if she'd won a lottery.

"Wow." Steve handed over her water bottle, eyes gleaming with approval. "Honey, you were on fire for the second half. What gives?"

She gulped some water and laughed. "It was a good set."

"A *good* set?" He shook his head admiringly. "It was the best I've ever heard you do. Let me buy you a drink."

She rolled her eyes at the familiar joke—drinks were on the house after the performance, and she and Steve always indulged in one together to wind down. "You're welcome to."

"Actually I was hoping for that privilege."

Lucy felt him behind her before he spoke; she gathered up her self-control and turned, smiling as if he were any old work buddy, grateful Steve would be around to dilute the tension. "Hey, Josh, glad you could make it."

"Josh, huh?" Steve sent Lucy a teasing glance. "I think I figured out why you were—"

"Josh Fairbanks." Lucy threw Steve a finish-that-sentence-and-die look and gestured toward her coworker, trying to look casual, trying not to notice Josh's biceps tightening the short sleeves of his blue polo shirt or the trim lines of his legs in black jeans. "He works on me at Stenk—*with* me at Stenkel, Webb and Reese."

Okay, just let her die now.

Josh chuckled and shook Steve's hand. "Great job tonight."

"Thank you." Steve glanced at Lucy and back at Josh. "Well. Have fun, you two. I have to get going home."

"You can't stay?" She sent Steve a pleading glance, which he ignored. *Et tu, Stevie?*

Count him in the Down on Link Club, too. He'd been encouraging her to move on for months. But he barely knew Link and had a weakness for big-eyed wiry brunettes like Josh.

"I'll call you." Steve kissed her cheek as an excuse to whisper, *Get him, tigress,* packed up his things and left her to the wolves. Or wolf. Or…Lord, she was confused.

"So how about that drink?"

"Oh…" She laughed and rubbed her bare arms, though she wasn't remotely cold. Standing next to him on an iceberg wouldn't be cold. Of course, she'd worn her itty bittiest black dress with the rhinestone trim, and of course she was regretting it now, because of course it would look as if she wore it for him so he'd get ideas….

Which, of course, she sort of did. And she'd sort of love to hear what those ideas might be.

"I guess a drink would be nice." She needed one, regardless. "A friendly one."

He rolled his eyes good-naturedly. "Am I going to have to fight the deep freeze much longer?"

She crossed her arms over her chest. As if it was only a matter of time before she thawed?

"Josh, I'm involved with—"

"Believe me, I know." He took her arm and escorted her over to the bar, gestured her onto a stool, took a seat next to her and turned with one of his beautiful baleful looks. "I'm sorry if I sounded—"

"Lucy, dear?" A couple of regulars came over and congratulated her on her set—Mr. and Mrs. Epstein, who'd been married longer than she'd been alive. She smiled and chatted politely, aware Josh was restless next to her, ordering himself another drink and champagne for her. The second they left, another couple stepped forward, then a single woman, then another couple who lingered, the husband telling too many stories about his wife's long-ago career before she finally pulled him away and Lucy was able to turn back to Josh.

"Do you have to put up with that a lot?"

Lucy shrugged, surprised he'd ask her that way. But then he doubtless didn't understand what a thankless job performing could be. She liked talking to her fans. Not much else about the business was that pleasant and immediately rewarding. "It goes with the territory."

"I guess. Anyway, as I was saying…" He stood, moved his stool closer to hers and sat again. "Well, let's drink first to tonight. You were fantastic."

"Thank you." She clinked her glass to his—looked like he was drinking whiskey, as her father did. "It was nice of you to come."

"I wanted to hear you sing. I wanted a taste of this other

side of you. It's…beyond fabulous." He took a swig of whiskey and put the drink on the counter, leaned close. "Do you have any idea how sexy you look up there?"

She blushed—of course she did, and where was her siren act now? "Wow. Thank you. I don't really know what to say."

"How about that you'll take a walk with me tonight?" He gestured toward the exit with his glass. "Somewhere, anywhere, so we can look at the stars."

She pictured it immediately—walking along the streets, frosty-breathed, maybe hand in hand, stopping to look at the stars, pointing out those they knew. Then his hand on the back of her head and another of those kisses that would burn her from the inside out.

"I can't."

He made a sound of frustration. "I'm trying to be patient, Lucy. But when I want something—or someone—the way I want you…"

"Please, Josh." She cringed. She was being ridiculously weak. Either she had to jump or pull back. It wasn't fair to Josh to keep him guessing like this. She just couldn't seem to make herself go either way.

"Okay." He picked up his drink and drained it. "I'm sorry, but I'm going crazy. You give me go signals all over the place and then I keep bouncing off the same barrier."

"I'm the one who's sorry, Josh." She put a hand on his shoulder, startled to find herself unfairly comparing it to Link's broader one. "It's me. I'm a mess right now."

"I am, too. I want you so much. But I know if I push too hard, you'll go running back to Link because it's safe with him." He leaned forward so his face was inches from hers. "I'm dangerous because your feelings for me are hot and confusing. Aren't they?"

She stared down at her knees and nodded. Barely.

"And your feelings for him are cool and calm and safe. Aren't they?"

She stopped another nod before it happened, feeling panic starting. "They're not safe. They're real."

"Then why are you here with me? Look at me, Lucy." He pulled her chin up so she had to look into his eyes, had to feel that attraction again. "*This* is real."

His mouth was on hers before she knew to stop him, a long, hot, wet kiss that traveled places no kiss on its own should travel with anyone but Link.

She pulled back and stared at him, breath coming too fast, starting to tremble. "No."

"God, Lucy, don't do this. Didn't you feel that?"

"I have to go." She fumbled frantically for her coat and purse, left the bar without even saying good-night to Dick, aware Josh was right behind her.

Outside in the icy air, he grabbed her arm, spun her to him and kissed her again, pressing her back until the outside brick of Eddie's cut into her back.

"This is real, Lucy." He grabbed her hips, drove his pelvis against her; she could feel him hard through his jeans and her thin dress.

"Please don't."

He stopped immediately, breathing hard. For a second she thought he was going to get angry with her.

Instead he moved back. Stroked her face with his thumbs. Kissed her gently again. "I'm sorry. I'll try to be patient. It's just…I'm sorry, I don't want to blow this. I'll walk you to your car."

"You don't have to."

"Please. Let me do something right."

She relented, let him help her with her coat and let him hold her hand in an awkward, miserable silence for the mercifully short trip to her beloved, familiar Mazda.

"Good night, Lucy." He kissed her again, apologized again.

She started the car and drove away, carrying a mental picture of him walking away, head bowed, hands jammed in his pockets.

Her heart ached, her head pounded…and the dark thrill of sexual excitement, the sense memory of his bulging fly pressing against her, wouldn't leave her alone.

Trouble with a capital T-R-O-U-B-L-E.

She needed to see Link. When she saw him everything would be clear. Her deep soul would speak to her—one way or another. All she needed was see him and she'd know what to do. She couldn't go on this way anymore, telling Josh yes with everything but her words. She owed it to him, to Link and to herself to make some kind of decision, take some kind of positive action instead of lying down and letting life walk all over her.

She reached Cambridge in fifteen minutes and parked on Garden Street. Marched firmly up the walk, into their building and up into their third-floor condo.

Link was up. The TV was blasting its usual deadening nonsense in the living room. She glanced in, but he wasn't there. "Link?"

"Yeah." His strong, deep voice came from the kitchen.

She walked lightly, arranged her features pleasantly, guilt warring with excitement.

"Hi."

He turned from the refrigerator where he was standing, door open, eating leftover potato salad out of the deli container with a fork. A blob of potato salad had caught on the bristles on his unshaven chin. "Hey, how was your show tonight?"

She stared. He was Link, as usual. Broad shoulders filling out his T-shirt, well-toned biceps emerging below, leading to strong forearms. Boxers, well-muscled legs, feet bare—did he ever get cold?

Link. Josh.

No clarity. Nothing. Her deep soul wasn't saying a blessed thing.

Figured. Krista's undoubtedly would have.

"Fine. The show was good tonight." She stepped forward and kissed him, tasting potato salad and the familiar—safe?—taste of Link.

"Want some?" He scooped up a forkful and squinted at her, mischief lighting his blue eyes. He knew how much she hated when he ate out of the container, not to mention that he left the refrigerator door open while he was doing it.

She laughed unwillingly, guilt sickening her even to the thought of food. "No, thanks. You going to bed soon?"

He shook his head. "Late movie, *Full Metal Jacket*. No way I'm missing it."

"Even if you get a better offer?" She lowered her voice, soft and sultry. See how her siren act worked on *him*....

Link looked at her strangely. "Like what?"

Lucy sucked in a breath, shocked at how much it hurt.

"Luce." He closed the refrigerator door and put down the potato salad, pulled her into his arms for a brief hug. "I was kidding. Lighten up."

"Sorry." She smiled, but her heart started cooling, along with her libido.

"I'd love to, but I'm... Long day, and my head is in the movie thing. I'm sorry."

She nodded. Not as sorry as she was, though she should have predicted it. Link was appallingly bad at switching gears, and if he'd planned a movie, nothing short of hurricane warnings would budge him—and maybe not even those. Not that she was Miss Spontaneity herself. She tried not to compare it to an invitation to walk under the stars.... "I understand."

She didn't. She didn't understand. They'd be spending yet another evening apart. The gulf between them had gotten so wide she didn't even know how to try anymore.

"You want to watch with me?" He chucked her under the chin and lifted his eyebrows hopefully.

Of course she didn't. She detested movies like that. He knew as much. "I think I'll turn in. But thanks. The chance to watch people blown to bits is really enticing."

He chuckled and leaned in for another potato-salad kiss. "Okay, puss. Sleep well."

She hated when he called her puss. "Don't call me that."

"All right." His expression turned defensive; he backed off. "Sorry. Sorry again. Sorry for everything."

She closed her eyes. "It's okay. I'm tired tonight. Maybe hormonal or something, too."

"Gotcha. Not a problem." His voice was forced cheerful, not that she blamed him.

"Good night." She turned and left the kitchen, hoping against hope he'd at least say something about her dress, about how great her ass looked in it walking away....

She turned the corner, glanced back and saw only his torso bent over, his head already back in the refrigerator.

Great. She followed the hallway to the bedroom she

shared with him. Showered, changed into her nightie and shut the bedroom door, grimacing at the machine gunfire noises coming down the hall from the TV.

Yeah, much more exciting than having sex with her.

In bed she tried to interest herself in a holiday catalog, in what to get her father—always the most difficult to shop for, anything to keep her mind off Link….

Who was she kidding? Off Josh. No luck. She couldn't concentrate. Finally she turned out the light and slid under the covers.

Immediately her traitor brain replayed the evening— the way Josh had looked at her, the way he'd kissed her, the way he'd pushed her against the building as if he was starving for her. As if his desire—and his heart—could barely be controlled.

She whimpered and her hand found its way down into her panties. She stroked there, imagining herself saying, *Yes, yes, please.* Imagining him taking her right there against the side of the building, in full view of passersby, strong and relentless, thrusting into her, riding her up the brick until she was nearly there, nearly there….

And then it was Link, not Josh, holding her, his bigger build, bulging muscles everywhere, his hips pumping her savagely.

Lucy shook her head in frustration. *No, no, this was her fantasy, for heaven's sake.* Please, at least let her cheat on Link in fantasy.

She forced Josh back into the scene, had Josh make love to her and made sure it was Josh's name that came to her lips when her orgasm swept through her.

Yes. She did it.

She let the bliss recede, fingering herself gently until the final shocks slowed and were past.

And then the moment she'd hoped for in the kitchen, the moment of clarity, hit her, so pure and perfect and simple that she couldn't believe she hadn't been able to get through to this place before.

She loved Link, but the thrill was gone. Krista was living a fantasy come true, a new wonderful lover in the mysterious dark of hotel rooms.

Why couldn't she? Without risking her life with Link. Have her cake and eat it, too?

She laughed and turned over, hugging her pillow to her chest and her new thrilling secret to her heart.

She, sensible, practical Lucy Marlow, was going to have an affair.

"WOMEN ARE SIMPLE." Seth's father gestured expansively with his walking stick, which he carried for show as far as Seth could tell since he'd recovered from his stroke. Speak loudly *and* carry a big one. "You find out what they want and give it to them. Shuts them up and makes life happy for everyone."

Seth rolled his eyes. He and his father were sharing his father's daily constitutional—out the door of the Joy Street condo he shared with his second wife, Aimee's mother, around the border of the Boston Common and the Public Garden and back home. "So it's fine if Aimee sells a billion copies of a piece of crap and God knows what else she'll cook up and still represents the stores?"

"Aimee's young. She's having fun. If she wants to write a book, let her. Believe me, you try standing in her way, you're asking for trouble. Her mother and I learned that a long time ago."

Because her mother and you never wanted to be bothered by anything as pesky as discipline.

"I don't want my rear end fried over this. I pushed Aimee at the board. A lot of them were hesitant enough even before this ludicrous stint at novel writing."

"The board is a bunch of old farts." He glanced sidelong at Seth. "I know because I'm one of them."

Seth chuckled and mumbled the obligatory remark about his father's vigor and youthful appearance.

"Well, thank you, son." His surprised pleasure seemed so genuine, Seth chided himself for being flip. His father was still thick-haired, trim and handsome, he'd recovered most of the strength on the left side of his body after his stroke and was able to set an unflagging pace on the one-and-a-half-mile walk every day, leaning on his stick only occasionally, using it to gesture often. So far he'd made no noises about his return as CEO of Wellington, but Seth expected the rumbles to start any day.

"So you don't see the book causing problems for the stores' image?"

"You wanted young and hip, that's what you're getting."

"True." Seth chose to ignore the drip of acid in his father's tone. "But I didn't want young and hip and laughing stock."

"She won't be. Although…"

His father loved trailing off, cueing questions from his listeners. Seth curbed his impatience. "Although what, Dad?"

"So far Aimee's antics have been played on the local scene—that disgraceful cult hit album she put out, the part in *Sweatshock*—she's still a Boston phenomenon. Being the spokeswoman for Wellington will take her throughout New England, possibly farther, which means certain of her critics will gain a wider and louder mouthpiece, especially after the press conference tomorrow."

"True." Seth braced himself. He could see this particular train wreck coming a mile away. The board obviously had his father's ear on the topic of Krista.

"You know this Marlow woman?"

"I know of her." He kept his voice casual, pretending fascination with the holiday storefronts along Tremont Street.

"She gets yammering loud enough, too many people are going to start listening. Local newspapers are one thing, but the whole world has access to the Internet. I don't want her garbage ruining the announcement of this change. Fine if she keeps the criticism to Aimee's questionable acting, singing and writing skills, but I don't want to hear a word against our stores from that bitch."

Seth opened his mouth. The hot rush of annoyance had been instant; he was ready to draw a sword and defend Krista's honor, when he knew by now it was easier to agree with his father and then do or think whatever he wanted on his own.

He closed his mouth and waited until his anger cooled.

"In general, Dad, I'd say the more publicity, the better. Even a little controversy can help." They rounded the corner from Tremont onto Boylston, toward the corner onto Arlington, home to the Ritz-Carlton where he and Krista had spent several passionate hours last week. He couldn't help smiling, replaying a few key moments....

"Every wagging tongue is another wag that keeps the Wellington name in people's minds?"

"Exactly." He was surprised to find himself replaying more of their conversation than sex. When had he felt so comfortable talking to a woman? Or to anyone since he'd lived with Hank that summer in Maine, nearly two years ago. Didn't say much for his romantic choices or the friends he surrounded himself with. He and Mary had been all about sex. Other women since college had barely made an impression—at least intellectually. On the road, then back here in his corporate life, he hadn't had many opportunities to forge long-lasting friendships.

Or maybe he'd squandered them.

"As long as she keeps her viciousness away from the stores and the Wellington name as a whole."

"Yes." They passed the Ritz and Seth stopped his train of thought. What the hell was he doing thinking about Krista in terms of a long-lasting friendship? He'd managed two incredible encounters in total darkness without letting on who he was. But already the strain was showing. When they'd parted at the Ritz, the will-I-see-you-again question had hung thick as mist in the darkness between them.

The answer was no, it had to be no, but the power of their encounter still held him, and he'd asked for some way to contact her directly. She'd given him an e-mail address she used when she wanted to be anonymous, with no hint of her name.

Perfect. Except why the hell had he even been thinking of e-mailing her?

Because the second she'd left, all the life and magic and energy in the room had gone with her. Turning on the light and illuminating the luxurious anonymity of a hotel room had been the final blow.

Back then, standing in the black hole of her absence, the scrap of paper she'd scrawled her address on in the dark had felt like a blessing. Like the glass slipper Prince

Charming clutched at the ball after Cinderella fled. He knew he held not a shoe but a means to find her again.

And then what?

"The sad truth is that people are idiots." Seth's father sent a flock of pigeons fluttering with his stick. "They'll undoubtedly love the book no matter what reviewers say or no matter how bad it is."

"Undoubtedly."

From e-mail, one short step to a phone number. Krista Marlow wasn't Mary. She wasn't a woman he could evict from his brain when she was out of the room. When she'd surrendered so completely to his tongue and fingers, gone so quiet and still, become so accepting and open in body and mind, they'd connected on a much deeper level than sexually. She'd been as shaken as he was, wanted to leave, wanted to stay, exactly as he felt. In the end they'd both chosen to stay, tangled under the covers, talking, until her nearness and scent had driven him to make love to her again, slowly and intensely. And if he'd been shaken once before, he was twice after.

Krista wasn't the kind of woman who would bore him after a few times together. The more frequently they corresponded, the more frequently they met, the harder it would be to either end it or reveal himself, which of course boiled down to the same thing.

Selfishly he wasn't ready to give her up. Holding back felt wrong, moving forward felt wrong—and standing still wasn't his style.

"...but this Marlow woman..."

Seth jerked himself out of his thoughts and tuned into what his father was saying.

"...there's something about her I really dislike. Sarcasm is not attractive in a woman. Gossip either." He turned and regarded Seth solemnly from under his graying eyebrows. "That's one thing about your mother, son, she never had a harsh word for anyone."

Seth accepted the compliment to his mother, glad his father hadn't been around to hear what she had to say after he'd dumped her for a trophy bimbo.

"Krista Marlow manages to be downright unfeminine. Her rants are ugly and personal. Good criticism doesn't stoop to that level."

Seth nodded automatically, trying to wrap his brain around *Krista Marlow* and *unfeminine* in the same sentence and failing.

"What does that woman have against Aimee?"

Seth shrugged. "Probably the same thing many people do. That Aimee has the world at her feet and doesn't deserve to."

His father indulged in The Frown, the expression that sent little boys and grown men alike scurrying for safety. "I'm surprised at you, son, talking about a family member like that."

Seth peered ahead, measuring the distance, ready for the walk to be over. Right. Family. The accidental genetic glue that bound people together for all eternity. "Sorry, Dad. But Aimee's a walking target."

"Maybe." He sighed and touched the brim of his fedora to an elderly lady passing with her poodle. "Probably."

They turned the corner onto Beacon Street, past the bar that inspired the old *Cheers* television series and up the hill toward Joy Street.

"I'm thinking…"

Cue question. Seth dutifully complied. "Yes, Dad?"

His father turned and regarded Seth seriously. "I'm thinking that Marlow woman needs to get laid."

Somehow Seth managed to keep his burst of laughter down to a chuckle, but that's as far as he could contain it. Luckily his father joined in.

"You know what I mean, son?" His father thumped him on the back. "You can always tell the bitter spinsters, huh?"

"Sure, Dad." He grinned. He and his dad had little in common, but every now and then he felt the father-son bond, even when he couldn't agree with much that came out of Seth Wellington III's mouth.

"You need to find out what her problem is." Seth Wellington III punctuated this pronouncement with sharp jabs of his stick on the sidewalk.

"*I* need to?"

"You or I or whoever. Find out her problem with Aimee. With life. With her hormones. Whatever it is. We're announcing Aimee as spokesperson tomorrow afternoon and we need her to back off before the reopening next week. Before those commercials launch. Media will be swarming."

"I doubt we'll be able to stop her. I think it would be unwise to get involved."

"Gotta get your feet dirty sometime, son."

Seth turned to him with narrowed eyes. "Meaning?"

"Wade into the muck, wrestle in it, get a mouthful and see how it tastes. You're an observer, son, always have been."

A slow burn started in Seth's gut. Damn it, he'd given up the life he wanted to live for his father's passion and his father's dream and his father had the balls to criticize him for it?

He swallowed the temptation to light into dear old dad

and concentrated instead on the last few yards remaining before they could go their separate ways.

"All right." His father's tone softened, all the apology Seth would ever get. "But I think she needs to be dealt with one way or another."

Dad was right. But in ways he would never suspect. "If we contact her, we risk antagonizing her further."

"Nonsense. She can't *go* much further before she's liable for slander." He chortled and rubbed his hands. "Possibly we could nail her with a lawsuit. I'll check into it."

Seth shook his head. "She'd make public our attempts to shut her up. Then the board looks as foolish as Aimee."

They reached the bottom of Joy Street. At long last. Seth's father stopped and turned.

"I doubt that, Seth. Everyone has a price. You need to find out what this woman's deal is, find out what she wants." He reached forward and jabbed Seth's shoulder. "And then, son, all you have to do is find some way either to give it to her or convince her she'd be much happier without it."

9

December 15

OH GOODY. I CAN HARDLY contain my delight today. Seriously. Someone hold me down before I start gamboling about my apartment.

Aimee Wellington is going to write a novel!

Finally, finally, dear fans, we will all be able to read about—I quote—"like…my life, but not really."

This is good! This is wonderful! Fans of fiction should be rejoicing everywhere at the chance to be able to read about, like … her life, but not really. At long last we can stop suffering through the tepid tedious prose of the masters and read a work by this woman, who is clearly a brilliant wordsmith.

For your reading pleasure, I quote again some choice pearls. "It's going to have some, like, adventure and some stuff like that, you know, danger…and yeah, maybe even probably some sex in it, too."

Followed by rapid girlish giggle and extended hair toss.

Followed by your blogger's rapid greenish gargle and extended cookie toss.

But wait! There's more! All those of you who stupidly bothered graduating from an institute of higher learning and/or have wasted time and money on the clearly ludicrous step of studying creative writing, who have slaved feverishly over your brilliant works only to encounter rejection after rejection or a luke-warm sale with a low advance that barely earns out, rejoice! Because there's more for you to choke on!

Ms. Wellington's advance is reputed to be…wait for it…

God, no, it's such a travesty I can't even bring myself to write it.

Way, way too much.

A dollar-fifty would be too much. The publishing world is bestowing an advance of six—count 'em and weep, fair readers—six big fat figures that would do the world so much more good donated to public schools, with instructions that kids be taught not to read crap like Aimee Wellington's book.

Which, incidentally, she wanted titled "Aimee Aimée" ("ay-mee, ay-may"), which means Aimee Beloved, which means this blogger is heading for the toilet once again because one cookie toss simply wasn't enough.

NEWS FLASH: Through an exclusive and utterly fictional arrangement with her publisher, we are able to excerpt her novel right here, right now, for those too curious to wait until it's on the shelves.

Chapter One.

In which I am, like, born and everything.

So I was completely born on June nineteenth? Icky stuff, you totally don't want to hear about that.

And then my mother dressed me in this really cute outfit. And I was like so, so adorable and I know because I totally have pictures to prove it. And the silver spoon is right there in my mouth, too, because Daddy put it there for my very firstest picture ever! Which is right on this cute little page.

Wait, I'm bored, that was so much work, can I go shopping now?

Chapter Two next time. Until then, get real!

KRISTA PICKED A BOX of kids' breakfast cereal off one of the lower shelves at her neighborhood Stop & Shop. The sugariest stuff was always there, bang at eye level for nagging little ones trailing mom.

Krista wanted to propose a "cranky consumer" column to *Woman's Week* magazine, and what better place to start than in the cereal aisle? A small serving of some of these horrors contained a full tablespoon of sugar, nearly half the calories of the meal. Why not just sell vitamin-fortified sugar cubes and be done with it? She could start with cereal, then move on to the trend of disguising candy bars as healthy snacks and... She glanced to the side, registering an intruder.

Um, hello? Stranger danger?

A very, very large man, dressed mostly in black leather, had come up to stand next to her, way too close, not moving, and though her glance barely took him in, she had the distinct impression he was staring at her.

Unhappiness.

Too big for John Smith, plus his visual was provoking a negative ten on the bubbly attraction scale, which John's wouldn't.

She moved a step to the right, closer to cereals that promised to taste like a bowl full of cookies. And what mother in her right mind thought kids confusing meals and sweets was a good idea?

The man took a step to the right also and stood. Still close. Still silent. Still staring.

This was registering high on a different scale than bubbly attraction—the creepy creep scale.

She turned briskly and brandished the box between them, looking directly at him. To her surprise, his bearded face was mild and pleasant, his eyes dark and intelligent. The kind of guy you'd ask to wear the Santa suit at the Christmas party. "One of your favorites?"

He shook his head scornfully. "Too sugary."

She smiled and pointed past him. "All-Bran's down that way."

"Not sugary enough."

Well, then. She gave a thin smile and took three steps to her right this time, grabbing a box of cereal that promised to taste like a bowl full of donuts.

The large male body also took three steps to his right. Okay, now she was scared, Santa or no Santa. She turned again and took a step back. "Are you following me?"

"Yup."

"Why?"

"You Krista Marlow?"

She narrowed her eyes. "No."

"Right." He put beefy hands on meaty hips, which made his arms and chest look even larger. "What do you have against Aimee Wellington?"

Crap. Double crap. An obsessed Aimee fan. She didn't have time for this. Nor did she relish the idea of her lifeless body being found here clutching two cereal boxes she wouldn't be caught dead buying any other time. "Not a thing. Why?"

"Then why are you printing such garbage about her on your site?"

"What site?" For God's sake, get lost, big guy.

He moved a step closer; she barely managed to stand her ground, clutching the boxes to her body like shields.

"Don't play stupid. Why are you so insistent on taking her down?"

A mom and her kids came down the aisle, giving Krista courage. Didn't thugs have some mom-and-children code of honor? He wouldn't kill her in front of them. Would he? "Because she is exactly as necessary to our cultural and spiritual well-being as this cereal is to the growing body of a child."

Ha! That would stop him.

He shook his head, and Krista was struck again by how mellow he seemed in spite of his terrifying bulk. She didn't get the feeling he was wound up and dying to use his fists. A gentle giant? "She's just a kid."

"Then she should leave the grown-up stuff to the grown-ups."

He glanced at her cereal boxes and raised an eyebrow. "Uh..."

She wanted to roll her eyes. No matter what she said, she was going to sound like a guy claiming he bought *Playboy* for the articles. "It's for a column."

"Right."

"On how people are losing their taste for anything of quality because they're being force-fed crap by marketing and publicity machines."

His eyes narrowed. He got the connection. Definitely not a dummy. "Aimee is having fun. She's hurting no one."

"What about all the people who deserve what she has through talent and a lot of extremely hard work and years of paying their dues?"

His expression cleared. "Is that what this is? You know someone like that?"

Bingo. She shrugged, but she had a feeling she'd been outed by her own zeal. Though if he knew enough about her to find her in a grocery store—shudder—he probably knew a whole lot about her. And Lucy. And was probably toying with her right now. "Maybe."

"Look. I know she's had a lot of stuff easy that other people want. But she's had it tough, too. Money isn't everything. She's…" His face softened. "Searching. She's still trying to figure out who she is, apart from being a Wellington. It's hard because, being a Wellington, she has to go through the searching we all do—trying things out, making mistakes, trying something else—in public."

"She doesn't have to do it in public."

He shook his head as if Krista was too stupid to live, and she wished he was small enough to beat up. "Did you ever have a part in a high school play? College? What was the last one you did?"

She had to think. "Anita in *West Side Story*."

"And how good were you?"

"Merely adequate. But that's my point. High school or college theatre is an appropriate arena for that level of try-ing out, but—"

"You're telling me if some big shot had come up to you back then and said, hey, you're fantastic, we want you to star in our Broadway-bound show, you would have said no, sorry, I don't believe I've completed enough years of study to perfect my craft? At eighteen? Nineteen? Twenty-one?"

She blew out a breath, imagining the moment, able to picture her excitement perfectly. "No. Probably not."

"But somehow Aimee's supposed to have that kind of perspective." He scrunched his lips in disgust. "Just think about it. And go easy on the poor kid. She's crying every night because of the shit you say about her."

He turned and walked past her, pausing to grab a box of Shredded Wheat 'N Bran, glancing at Krista's sugar-coated sugar. "This is *her* favorite."

And a perfectly timed exit at the end of the aisle.

Ouch.

She stayed where she was for several minutes, ignoring curious glances from other shoppers, making sure Mr. Black Leather had plenty of time to pay for his healthy cereal and leave.

She couldn't say she was anxious to see him again.

Then she put her cereal back on the shelves and scooted out of the store, dropped a quarter in the Salvation Army bucket as she did every time she passed and started walking back down Cambridge Street toward Charles.

The air was cold and gray and damp; her mood plummeted to match. By the time she got home, it had started to sleet, a stinging, freezing, wet mess. Ho ho ho.

Perfect. Matched her mood.

Her apartment seemed dark and airless. She couldn't get the image out of her head of Aimee Wellington crying. Over something *she'd* said.

She pulled up her e-mail. Note from her editor at the *Sentinel*. Note from Lucy. Note from a college friend.

She pulled up her Hotmail account, the address she'd given John Smith.

Nothing. That made three endless days since their date at the Ritz on Monday and not a word from him.

Great. Just dandy. Never mind that her life had veered from thrills to satisfaction to loneliness and finally the threat of despair without him. But what did she expect from a fantasy lover? E-mails every hour?

Actually after their extraordinary date in the hotel room, the incredible ease and intimacy of their conversation and the passion of their lovemaking, she'd expected to hear from him soon, yes. By now she'd been reduced to her list of maybes. Maybe he was busy. Maybe he was out of town. Maybe he'd lost her e-mail address.

Maybe he wanted to be gone.

Well, fine. She'd be better off without him and those memories driving her crazy, keeping her up at night. The pain would subside. The feelings weren't real, they were based only on her ideal of who he could be.

Never mind that she'd connected with him on a more real level than any man she'd ever been with.

She turned on the TV, grabbed a bag of organic blue-corn tortilla chips and flopped down on her couch.

Nothing on. Soaps, local news, more local news and...

Whoa. She sat up straight, staring at the screen. Aimee freaking Wellington. At a press conference. Could Krista's day get any weirder?

No one answer that. Next to Aimee, a guy who looked extremely familiar. He was just stepping down from the microphone—where had she seen that face before?

Aimee got up to the podium, and Krista studied her, crunching chips thoughtfully. She was young. Very young.

Reading some prepared statement about how glad she
was to be representing her family's stores. All the while
looking as glad as if someone had stuck her full of pins.

Interesting. Krista wasn't going to start feeling sorry for
her yet, but this was definitely...interesting.

Aimee turned the microphone back to the gorgeous
guy next to her. He started speaking, but the announcer
took over immediately, wrapping up the commentary on
the company's announcement. New look, new image, blah
blah blah.

Krista stared at the man at the podium, still talking under
the drone of the announcer's words. He was so familiar. She
had seen him or someone that looked like him...where?

For the second before the shot switched back to the stu-
dio, he turned toward the camera and she got a glimpse of
his face at a different angle that placed him immediately.

She bounced back against the couch, chip halfway into
her mouth. No way. No way! Must be someone who
looked like him. Exactly like him. Freakily like him.

But for a crazy second she was positive he was the
water-spilling guy in the booth behind her and Lucy at
Thai Banquet two weeks ago. The guy who'd turned her
inside out with a look. The guy who had fled the restaurant immediately after she'd spotted him. Aimee's stepbrother, Seth.

Seth Wellington, sitting right behind her table while she
and Lucy had talked about relationships and Christmas
and Krista's personal sexual fantasy. Ack!

Wait a second. She crunched her chip slowly...
slower...stopped. Add to that the big guy today in the
grocery store and this all started feeling very, very wrong.
Where and who else? How many other times?

She swallowed her mouthful and closed the bag of chips, appetite gone.

Either she was getting extremely paranoid or the Wellington clan was keeping very close tabs on Krista Marlow.

LUCY SWIVELED BACK and forth in her office chair. If she was really going to do this, now was the perfect time. Her boss, Alexis, was out of the office in some important afternoon meeting. Most of her flunkies were out with her, including Josh. Lucy's area was empty. A lot of the rest of the staff was still at lunch. No one would disturb her or make unexpected demands on her time. She could make this happen exactly the way she wanted it to go.

So.

She'd lain awake most of last night and the night before that trying to figure out what to say, how to ask him. Worrying over the wording, worrying over possible responses.

Enough worrying, enough being so Lucyish. The situation was becoming desperate and she needed to act.

She pulled up an e-mail, unable to dispel the surreal feeling that this wasn't really happening, that she hadn't really been pushed to this point. And yet, if it helped dispel the boredom, helped eliminate the rut...

If this affair could only do that, then it was the best idea she'd ever had.

Would he be angry she was after an affair with him? Think she was crazy? Or—the part that scared her most—not be willing to risk it?

She tabbed past the To field, too nervous to put in his name yet in case she hit Send by mistake before she was ready. She'd done that once with a strongly worded e-mail to a girlfriend in an abusive relationship, changed her mind about sending it and instead of hitting Delete, made a horrible finger slip it had taken her a long time to apologize for. This way she'd have every opportunity to chicken out if she lost her nerve. Which could happen.

Yikes. She was a mess.

Why wouldn't she be? She didn't exactly initiate affairs every day. And she couldn't help feeling her entire future happiness rested on this decision and its outcome.

How to begin?

Hi.

Well, that was auspicious. A real attention grabber for sure. Now what? She closed her eyes, thought of Krista and her mystery man. Krista didn't sit around analyzing forever. She saw, she wanted, she went. Exactly what the love doctor ordered. Lucy craved that kind of excitement, that secret thrill of the forbidden. Things with Link were so stale now, it had been way too long since she'd felt that vitally alive.

I don't think it's any secret that I find you incredibly attractive. There have been times looking at you I am so overcome with lust, I can barely stand not ripping your clothes off and climbing all over you.

I won't pretend I'm not still deeply in love with the guy I live with. I am. But things have been rough between us lately. Something is missing and I don't know how to get it back. I don't think we are able to reconnect with what brought us together in the first place. Maybe it's crazy, but I thought this might help.

I want to have an affair with you. I want to meet

you at a hotel and do wild, lustful things to you until neither of us can stand up any longer. I want to see you lose control and I want to be the one making you do it, then I want to go home and think about you all night long, keep those memories with me during what has gotten to be a stale routine with my boyfriend.

I know this is crazy. You probably think I'm completely nuts. But I think we owe it to each other at least to try this.

Yours,

Lucy

She read it over, then again and once more, making sure the note said exactly what she wanted it to say as she'd planned it, seeing how it looked in the flesh, as it were, typed up and ready to go.

Yes. It did. Good.

Now or never…

Now.

She typed in the To column the name of the man she'd loved since she'd first set eyes on him so many years ago: Link Baxter. Sent up a brief prayer to God that the crazy scheme would work, that it would save them from the disintegration that had started to feel inevitable, that it would save her from the crazy, shallow temptation of Josh.

Link was and always would be the man for her. It was time she stopped whining and despairing and denying and did something about it. If Krista could make her fantasies come true, then Lucy could, too, with the man who at one time had been all of them come to life and who she believed deep in her soul could be all of them again.

She crossed her fingers, crossed herself...and hit Send.

To: Lucy Marlow
From: Link Baxter
Subject: Your e-mail
Lucy, what the hell is this?
Did you mean to send this to me?
Link

To: Link Baxter
From: Lucy Marlow
Subject: re: Your e-mail
Of course I meant to send it to you. You probably think I'm horrible. I've never cheated on my boyfriend before. But things are bad right now at home, and you make me so nuts it's like I have no other choice. I can't stop thinking about getting you alone and naked.
How about it?
Tomorrow, five-thirty at the motel down the street from your office building. I'll tell my boyfriend I'm working late. He's so into his own stuff these days, he barely notices if I'm there or not.
Don't say no...I have a list a mile long of things I want to do to you.
Lucy

To: Lucy Marlow
From: Link Baxter
Subject: re: Your e-mail
Whoa. Lucy, I'm sure you're wrong about your boyfriend. There's no way a man could not notice you.

Though I have to say, my girlfriend has been acting recently as if she'd like me to drop dead, to save her the trouble of dealing with me.

Let me think about this. I'm not the kind of guy who cheats...that is, I never have been before.

But you are temptation, Lucy Marlow. Serious temptation.

Link

To: Link Baxter
From: Lucy Marlow
Subject: re: Your e-mail
There's no way your girlfriend could want anything but to get closer to you, even if she might have a freaked-out way of showing it. She's probably just scared she's losing you.

But I have no fear and no inhibitions and I want you like crazy. Every possible way there is to have you.

Will you come?

Lucy

To: Lucy Marlow
From: Link Baxter
Subject: re: Your e-mail
Interesting about my girlfriend. I never thought about it that way. But if she loses me, Lucy, it will only be to you.

I want you too—this is crazy, but I'm starting to love the idea of having you in a motel. I'm hard right now at my desk, thinking about us together. If my boss comes over to talk to me, he'll think I'm surfing porn.

So yes, I'll come tomorrow....

But not as many times as you will.

Link

10

KRISTA TOSSED A NATURAL puffed-cheese snack back into the bag and wiped her crumby fingers on her second favorite old sweats, these baby-blue. She had all of two words typed onto today's blog: *Hello, all.* That took her about two seconds.

Then she'd sat there. And sat there. And sat there. Twice she actually typed a few more words. And deleted them.

This never happened unless she was stuck for subject matter, but that wasn't the case today. She'd promised her readers Chapter Two of the parody book by Aimee Wellington and...well, nothing was coming.

Scratch that, plenty was coming. Her usual sarcastic ranting, let's face it, the woman had *Please make fun of me* tattooed on her forehead.

But okay, that encounter with the guy in the supermarket had done two things. Given her a tiny whap on the head that yes, Aimee was a person. A young person. Who probably hadn't had the grounding in love and common sense that Krista and Lucy had had from their parents.

It had also given her the weird and doubtless paranoid feeling that she was being warned off. As in threatened. Why wouldn't Mr. Guy In Black just send her an e-mail through her site? Or call and leave her a message at the

Sentinel? Why track her down in her civilian life, standing in the cereal aisle? Of course, it could have been a coincidence that he'd shown up in the same aisle in the same
supermarket at the same time and recognized her, but it
was a whopper of one. Krista wasn't the kind of celebrity
people flagged down in public. He must have taken the
trouble to find a photo and study her face. And then the
way he'd just stood there and followed every step she'd
taken before speaking....

   She was creeped out. Add in the other "coincidence"
of Seth Wellington showing up at the same restaurant at
the same time, in the next booth, alone, where it would be
easy to stay silent and listen to her conversation. Add in
that he'd bolted the second she'd glanced at him long
enough to register his features and, for all he knew, his
identity. He wasn't as public as Aimee, but the Welling-
tons had been a premier Boston family for decades and
anyone who cared or paid attention to society stuff would
undoubtedly recognize him.

   In a desperate flash, she wanted the quiet strength and
reassurance of John Smith and just as quickly shook her
head. As if he was someone she could count on? Mr. Disappear and Reappear and Disappear again? Sure, he'd
taken a lot of trouble to assuage her fear in Maine, but then
he'd wanted in her pants. Sure, the time they'd spent together had been so intense she'd been stupid enough to develop feelings or think she was developing feelings, stupid
enough to grieve his loss as hard or harder than much
longer relationships she'd had.

   In this strange, vaguely threatening situation, why
wasn't she longing for Lucy or her mom and dad or her
close friends from college?

She didn't even know the guy's real name. Had never even seen him.

None of that helped. She wanted him with a fierce, determined passion that was freaking her out.

Her phone rang, and she pooh-poohed the adrenaline fear rush, picked it up and spoke firmly.

"Krista. It's Lucy."

"Lucy, what's up?" Krista got out of her chair and frowned. Her sister never called during the day and she sounded pretty worked up.

"First, I thought of the perfect present for Mom and Dad. A dinner and overnight at the Copley Plaza. What do you think?"

"Wow, that's a fabulous idea." Krista laughed good-naturedly. She could think all year long and never come up with ideas like Lucy. Christmas was about love—granted, this was an extremely expensive way to celebrate love, but why the heck not? "I'll go in on it with you for sure. It's perfect. They never spoil themselves."

"They'll have a blast. And Krista—" Lucy's voice dropped to a heavy whisper "—you're not going to believe this."

"What? Can you talk louder? I'm not going to believe what?"

"I can't talk louder, I'm at work, but I couldn't wait to tell you. I'm going to have an affair! With—"

"Oh my God." Immediately following the shock came a tidal surge of protectiveness for Link, the very guy she'd been urging her sister to leave. What had gotten into Lucy? "Are you sure Josh is worth this? Shouldn't you break up with—"

"No, not with Josh."

"There's *another* one?" Krista gasped. Link did not deserve this. Her sister had lost her mind.

"*No,* will you *listen* to me?"

"I'm listening." She stopped pacing opposite her window and stared nervously out at the quaint brick storefronts of Charles Street.

"I'm going to have an affair with Link."

"What? Who?" Krista's eyebrows drew down. "With *Link?*"

"Yes, isn't it crazy? I propositioned him and asked if he wanted to cheat on me with me and said I wanted to cheat on him with him, and he said yes." Her sister giggled madly, sounding happier than Krista had heard her in months, maybe years. "We're leaving work early to meet at the Cambridge Motel. I'm so excited! It's like we're going on our very first date all over again."

Krista's downed brows shot back up. Her mouth opened and she started to laugh, only the laugh came out half-assed because she was suddenly sick with envy. Not only her parents but her sister, too. A whole family of hotel trysters, only theirs were in the context of real, healthy relationships. She shoved the dark feeling away. This was not about her. "Lucy, that is hysterical! What a fabulous idea. You are a genius."

"Thanks. I'm really crossing my fingers this works." Lucy's voice dropped into a low, emotional zone. "I love this man, Krista. I don't want Josh except in some silly hormonal way, like when you have a crush on a movie star or someone you don't know."

Krista turned away from the window, the dark feeling rising again. Yeah, she could relate. In fact, too well. Her entire love life at the moment consisted of a crush—only it felt like more, but that was probably fantasy, too—on someone she didn't know. "It will work, Lucy. If he agreed to try it, he's got to be willing to meet you halfway."

"I think so, too. I'm so thrilled! I haven't felt like this since... Oh, hell, my boss is here. Gotta go. 'Bye!"

Krista punched off the phone and set it back into the cradle. Paced her apartment and picked up a picture of her family on vacation in Washington, D.C., when she and Lucy were teenagers. Her mom and dad had their arms around each other, grinning; she and Lucy were smiling at the stranger who volunteered to take the family portrait—a loving, close American family.

She put the picture down, ridiculously lonely. And now that she thought about it, she was also being whiny, which wasn't like her at all. She was a woman of action, and right now her next act wasn't at all clear.

She didn't like unclear.

Lucy was going to have an erotic adventure all her own. But with someone she trusted absolutely. Someone she knew inside out. Someone she loved to such a degree that she'd rather wallow through barnyards of muck trying to find a way to higher ground next to him, than take a simple sidestep and be high and dry easily, either on her own or next to someone new.

And—here came the whiny part—Krista, if she was very lucky, would get one more night or maybe two of anonymous sex with a man who didn't want her to know who he was, for reasons he didn't want to tell her.

Not only that, if she kept on her current path of holding Aimee up to anything resembling standards, she could get her kneecaps split by Mr. Black Leather, no doubt acting on orders from Mr. Privilege himself, Seth Wellington.

A vision of the press conference showed up right on

cue, and turned on the proverbial lightbulb. Of course. Now that Wellington had unveiled the empire's new direction with Aimee in the visible lead, the family and corporate big guys would go to any length to keep negative publicity away from her.

Which made Krista's position all the more complicated. If she continued to blast Aimee, she might be making powerful enemies. If she backed down, she'd be implicitly condoning exactly the kind of pandering she detested the most.

An animated buzzing fly announced the arrival of an e-mail. From Lucy. Apologizing for cutting her off.

She smiled at her sister's excitement and impulsively checked her Hotmail account.

Oh my God.

An e-mail from John. It had come in last night and she'd promised herself to stop checking so obsessively, so she hadn't seen it until now.

Hey, I've been massively busy the last few days, but you're on my mind—as usual. What's new?

A slow burn of pleasure started in Krista's belly. It wasn't over. She was on his mind...*as usual.* She'd get to see him again and...

Not see him.

She frowned and stared at the e-mail. What was new? She wanted to tell him. She wanted to tell him all of it and hear his reactions and his thoughts and feel his strong arms around her again. Not to mention have him take her to heaven and back a few times while she did the same for him.

But what did any of it mean, really? It was anonymous sex in the dark.

She wanted more.

The thought popped into her head as if it had been dictated by her subconscious and shot through a hole of denial into her brain.

She stood, paced around her living room, stopped by the window again and noticed an actual patch of blue sky. Glanced at her watch. Nearly two. Soon Lucy would be packing up for her tryst with Link. What would John Smith be doing? Did he work in an office? Would he pack up and go home to his wife and kids? To a lonely apartment? To a fabulous condo or a house in the burbs?

She wanted to know.

She whirled around, sat back down at her computer and, before she could have second thoughts, hit the reply key on his e-mail, typed in her cell number and clicked Send.

There. If he was sincere and single, he'd call. If he wasn't, he'd disappear.

So all she had to do was wait.

Easy.

Not.

Half an hour later, still no blog written, entertaining the idea of pulling out every one of her hairs one by one, she thought getting out of the house for a nice brisk power walk was probably a better idea, winter's chill be damned. Cell phone with her, of course.

So shoot her, she was weak.

Five minutes of power walking and then power walking wasn't enough, so she broke into a jog, enough nervous energy going to run the Boston marathon, around the Public Garden, then left on Beacon, crossing Storrow

Drive on the pedestrian bridge, then jogging along the Charles River, her body warming slowly.

Approaching the Harvard Bridge, it happened. Her cell rang. Number blocked.

"Hello?" She slowed to a walk, trying to keep her panting in check. *Pleeeeez, oh, pleeeeez.*

"You sound out of breath." A deep, dark, sexy, familiar voice.

Ohhhhh, extreme happiness.

"Hi."

"You in the middle of someone?"

She laughed too loudly, puffing clouds of steam, feeling too happy. Hell, even the sun was about to come out. "No, no, I'm out running."

"Should I call back?"

"No." She rolled her eyes at her panicking eagerness. She was more nervous than when Ralph Press called her in sixth grade. "Now is good. Now is really fine."

"Okay. How was your week?"

"It was...pretty... Well, there were...I mean... It was okay." She smacked herself on the head and got a strange look from a mom pushing a bundled up baby in a stroller. Oh, *that* was coherent. And pretty much summed up her feelings. She wanted to tell him everything, wanted to reach out, but how? She'd given him her number. He'd blocked his.

"I don't think I'm getting the whole story there."

She laughed uneasily. "It's complicated."

"I've got time. Meet me in an hour?"

Krista came to an abrupt stop, while her adrenaline took off racing ahead of her. He wanted to meet with her? So he could hear about her bad week? Would they meet in public this time, maybe over a drink? "Where?"

"The Ritz."

Her adrenaline backed off. In a hotel room. Again. In the dark. "You have a standing reservation?"

He chuckled. "If you say yes, I don't care how full the hotel is. I'll get one."

She laughed, not really amused, horrified at how much she'd wanted the date to be about sitting at a café at Quincy Market, sharing a beer and people watching, about unburdening herself to him and having him not only listen but hear her. Sex was great, she liked sex, particularly with him, she liked sex. But…

Oh, she was so getting herself in trouble here.

"I guess I better say yes." Her voice came out a husky whisper, which wasn't as much about erotic promise as it was about disappointment.

"I'll leave the room number for you at the front desk." His voice dropped, too, but she doubted for the same reason.

"For Jane Doe?" She grimaced. Might as well have *affair* tattooed on her forehead.

"Good point. I'll call you when I have a room and let you know the number."

"Deal." She waited for him to sign off. And waited. "Okay, I'll—"

"Is something wrong?"

Krista closed her eyes, fighting back a tear. He could read her moods even over the phone. Why were they wasting something this special in the dark?

"No. No." She forced enthusiasm back into her voice. "It sounds great. See you soon."

"Okay, Jane Doe. Soon."

She hung up, her thrill forever tarnished. So much for

her perfect fantasy. She should have left it alone—maybe she should have let him go that first night at the Pine Tree Inn. Maybe she should have obeyed her instincts in the hall outside their room at the Ritz and fled.

Her perfect fantasy had the possibility of being so much more to her.

She just wasn't sure it could ever be more to him.

THE OPERATOR AT THE Ritz came on the line and greeted Seth pleasantly. He opened his mouth to make the reservation, hesitated…then shook his head. "Sorry, wrong number."

He punched off his phone and got up from his desk, paced the spotless gray office carpet moodily, feeling caged and restless. He'd learned over the years to trust his instinct, and his instinct was telling him the Ritz-Carlton might be one of Boston's finest hotels, but it wasn't where he wanted to meet Krista tonight.

So where did he want to meet her? Or did he want to meet her at all? Was this hesitation his conscience knocking on his skull, asking how long he planned to mislead her? Or a simple been-there-done-that, time-to-move-on guy thing.

Not the latter. The idea of being with Krista still excited him. Hell, it consumed him. But seeing her…

No, it was *not* seeing her that didn't appeal anymore. He loved the feel of her, the smell and the sound and the taste of her. But that remaining sense was begging to be in on the action.

What that meant, he didn't care to examine. Easier to pretend it was some lust-driven ego-feeding need to be able to watch while he made her come. Easier to discount the rush of protective concern when he sensed her week had left her feeling down, maybe vulnerable, maybe confused. He hadn't planned to see her tonight; he'd just been e-mailing to see how she was, and when she'd sent her phone number...

He stopped opposite the window and put his hands to his hips, pushing back his jacket, staring at the sun glinting off the building opposite. Right. Just calling to see how she was. No intention of seeing her. Who was he kidding?

Not even himself any longer.

The phone rang and he rolled his eyes. Could these pesky business matters please stop interfering with his obsession?

"It's Mary. Did you happen to check Krista Marlow's blog today?"

"No." His apprehension rose. Just a feeling...but a bad one.

"There's nothing there but posts from people wondering where she is. No Chapter Two."

"Really." He sank back into his seat, the bad feeling intensifying. "Any guesses?"

"None. She was on a roll with the parody. People loved it and were clamoring for more. I've never seen so many reactions posted. Maybe she's ill? If she's going to be on the road she lets people know."

"You've been following her that closely?"

"Guilty." Mary let out a low laugh. "Count me among her fairly huge cult following. She cracks me up. And at the risk of sounding disloyal, most of the time she's right on."

"Tell me about it." He blew out a breath, feeling slightly sick. Something about this bothered him a lot, and he wasn't even sure why exactly. Why would she suddenly stop her crusade? And why had she sounded upset on the phone?

Two possible reasons tapped him figuratively on the

shoulder. On the right, a reason named Aimee, and on the left, dear old pater, Seth Wellington, III.

Aimee had turned Juice loose on Krista once before. Seth's father had been talking lawsuits and interference, words Seth had ignored. He didn't love what Krista's column might do to Wellington, but she did have a right to her opinion.

Had Aimee gotten fed up and struck again? Had his father gone ahead with some other form of intimidation?

The slightly sick feeling in his stomach turned hot and strong and angry and he banged his hand on the desk and shoved his chair back to stand. Damn it. He should not be this involved emotionally with a woman who had every reason to distrust him.

But in the words of Krista, *Get real, Seth*. Too late for that.

"Thanks for letting me know, Mary. Let's hope she lays off from now on."

"I'll miss it if she does. But yeah, the company comes first. I'll let you know if there are any new developments."

He thanked her and hung up. Strode to his office door, leaving a mountain of paperwork and unanswered mail on his desk. "Sheila, I'm leaving early today. Anyone needs to reach me, they're out of luck."

"Yes, sir." Her arched eyebrows asked the question for her.

He couldn't help a smile. "Personal time."

"Delighted." Her still-lovely face broke into an answering smile. She reached for a paper and held it out to him. "Before you go, I have a list of presents for your family. Did you want to check it or shall I go ahead?"

Seth took the list and scanned it quickly. Expensive. Tasteful. Impersonal.

Impulsively he handed the paper back. "Hold off, Sheila. I might want to take a closer look. Maybe see if I have any input."

"I will." Her smiled turned into an approving grin. "See you tomorrow."

Seth nodded, feeling pleased and satisfied. Maybe his Grinch heart had grown one size bigger.

He exited his outer office and strode down the corridor to the elevator, greeting employees curtly to discourage conversation. CEO on an Important Mission. In the company garage, in his car, he pulled out his cell, dialed Krista without even being certain of what he wanted to say, how he'd put it or what her reaction would possibly be.

All he knew was that he wanted to be with her, hear her voice, find out what was bothering her and test out these strange new feelings he'd had the idiocy to develop. Which meant he sure as hell wouldn't be meeting her at the Ritz.

And maybe not even in the dark.

"GOING SOMEWHERE? Maybe my way?"

Lucy jumped and nearly dropped her purse at the sound of Josh's voice. Oh, great. Now she was feeling guilty for going out with her own fiancé.

"I have a date." She tried not to speak primly, but she sort of did anyway and found it harder than usual to look him in the eye.

"You're leaving early for a date?" His dark raised brows clearly said *What, not with me?*

"With…Link." She was blushing madly—sheesh, how did women ever manage to juggle two men?

"Oh." His face fell. He took a step toward her, which made her glance nervously back into the hall behind her office. "So I guess going out with me again tonight is not going to happen?"

"No." She managed to look into his eyes then, and her insides didn't do cartwheels this time, only a sad, tired jitterbug. She'd made the right choice. "Not any night, Josh. I'm sorry."

He looked incredulous, took another step, which made her feel crowded and anxious. What was he going to do, try to kiss her right here at work?

"You're going to throw away *this?*" He leaned forward; she put a hand up to block him.

"Stop, are you crazy?" she whispered.

"Crazy for you, Lucy Marlow." He breathed the words out in a low, husky murmur. "You didn't stop me the other night."

"Actually...I did." She felt a surprising jab of irritation. Why hadn't she ever noticed all his lines sounded right out of a made-for-TV movie? "And I'm saying it now again. I'm sorry. I admit I was attracted to you—"

"Not was." He winked an Orlando Bloom eye. "You're still attracted to me. I can see it in your beautiful blues."

Oh, brother. Why hadn't she noticed sooner? The fantasy of the sexy stranger was Krista's, not hers. She could barely restrain her impatience to be out of this office and on her way to meet Link. But she owed Josh more than that.

"I know I led you on. I didn't mean to, I was genuinely confused. But you and I..." She shook her head, suddenly calm and sure, and looked him dead-on without flinching. "This is nothing I can pursue, Josh. I'm sorry. That's final."

He smiled with a touch of smugness, touched her hair and didn't even falter when she moved her head out of reach. "What's between us won't go away. I'll wait for you, Lucy..."

She anticipated his next words, and listened to them fall out of his mouth with a combination of horror and amusement.

"...forever if I have to."

Based on what? Good chemistry—okay, great chemistry but fading already—a couple of conversations, a nice kiss or two and a lot of meaningless googly-eye-making?

Her fault for being so mixed-up and vulnerable. She'd led him on more than she ever should have, but he had not the beginning of a clue about love. "Josh, in all fairness, I think you'd be better off finding someone—"

"Hey, Josh, there you are." Alexis Webb walked out of her office, tall, red-haired and perfectly turned out as usual, and handed him a file. "Here are the foreclosure notices on the Glickman case you said you needed back ASAP."

Lucy stiffened. Alexis flicked a glance at her and another one at Josh, who smiled as if they were all in on a big sexy joke together.

Lucy wanted to growl at him. Alexis better not think she was carrying on an affair with a colleague. Especially now, when she'd finally made it clear she'd never have one.

"Great, yeah, okay." He took the file and backed toward the exit with puppy-love eyes trained on Lucy. "Catch you later, Luce."

She cringed at his use of the nickname. He'd never catch her, later or ever. She was embarrassed even to have been tempted by his bait.

"So, Lucy, did I...interrupt anything?" Alexis was a total go-getter, one of the most direct and honest people Lucy had ever met. She probably ate men like Josh for practice.

"Nothing I didn't want interrupted."

Alexis smiled, obviously relieved. Did *she* want him? "I've known Josh a long time, Lucy. Good guy, great at his job. But his…tragic flaw, if you will, has always been falling for unavailable women."

"Really." She held herself still and calm, but there was no use trying to stop it. The blush was so fierce on her face Alexis would have to be an idiot not to notice. And Alexis was hardly that.

"I thought he might have been hitting on you?" She smiled and laid a friendly hand on Lucy's shoulder. "A couple of women have ended relationships because of him. They date for a while and then—oops—something goes wrong for him and he breaks it off. Hard to watch because I like and respect him. It's a pretty unhealthy pattern."

Lucy's blush cooled in a hurry. Unhealthy was right. And unhealthy was exactly what Lucy was feeling at that moment. "I'm not at risk. But thanks for telling me, Alexis."

"Sure." She gave Lucy a sly smile. "I've met your Link at various office parties and I'll tell you, he is…well…"

Lucy grinned as Alexis started fanning herself. "Way hot?"

"Just take care of him, because if I ever hear he's free …"

Lucy laughed, swelling with stupid territorial pride. He Tarzan. She Jane. "He's permanently taken."

"I figured. Have a good evening."

"Thanks, Alexis." Lucy smiled warmly, thinking Alexis had no idea how good of an evening she was going to have. "And thanks for the warning."

"No problem." She dumped a file in Lucy's in-box and walked back toward her office. "Glad it was unnecessary."

It damn well was. Lucy grabbed her jacket and her

purse and hightailed it to the bathroom, where she changed into a tight black miniskirt, high black heels and a tight low-cut red top. She wrapped her sensible raincoat around her and shot out of the office to her car, giddy with relief when she managed to avoid bumping into Josh again. She'd been so stupid to—

Okay, she needed to stop beating herself up so much. Not stupid. She was starving for what Josh had promised—only thank God she'd realized in time that she was starving for it from Link.

She drove to the motel, heart thudding, nervous as if this was their first date instead of their sixth year together. Yesterday at home, after dinner, when she'd casually dropped that she'd be working late tonight and he'd casually dropped that he was planning to go out for drinks with the guys, she'd had to turn away to keep from laughing. Their conversation had been of the pleasant how-did-your-day-go variety, but underneath it crackled a current of excitement that hadn't been there in way, way too long.

And under the sexual anticipation lay another layer— the warm thrill that Link was in this with her one hundred percent. That he wanted to fix their relationship, not coast by on indifference, as so many couples did, or let love fade into an ugly—or worse, disinterested—breakup.

She pulled into the parking lot, laughing out loud, hoping he'd already gotten the room, because even though they were a legitimate couple of the age of consent, she'd probably blush like mad and overexplain to the desk clerk.

Her laughter died when she saw Link, replaced by a jolt of chemical excitement.

Oh my God. If Josh had looked like a puppy before, he looked like a toy one now.

Link was leaning against his beloved Honda convertible, jeans covering long, strong legs crossed at the ankles, arms folded across a T-shirt-covered chest, the dark blue bomber-style jacket she'd bought him last Christmas and his black Ray-Ban sunglasses giving him a tough-guy look that was making it hard for her to breathe.

He was so sexy. They hadn't made love in weeks, and she suddenly felt the deprivation of every single one retroactively. No, of every single day.

Rapidly approaching every single hour.

She parked across the lot, opened the door and let her long dancer legs emerge first, making sure her coat was open so he'd get the full view when she stood. She wasn't the miniskirt-and-high-heels type. Or never had been before. She prayed the view would have the effect she wanted.

It did. He stared, then looked her slowly up and down from behind those hot Ray-Bans, a smile curving his firm masculine lips.

She slammed the car door and prowled toward him, walking like a model on a runway, letting the coat flap open.

Three steps away, he lifted one arm toward her, smile turned mischievous, a key dangling off the end of his finger. "Home, sweet home. Room 212. Nonsmoking."

"Perfect."

He flipped the key around, reached and spanned her waist with his large hands, pulled her forward so she had to straddle his legs and lean full against him.

She wasn't complaining. He bent down so his lips were less than an inch from hers.

"I've been thinking about nothing but this all day."

"Me, too." Her words came out breathy and silly. Her mouth was on fire for him to kiss her, as if he were really her forbidden lover, as if this was really their first time. Under her coat, his hands explored the short skirt, moving over familiar territory as if it was a new landscape to him, too.

Her hormones went wild. "Link…"

"I know. Let's go." He grabbed her hand and pulled her, walking so fast she practically had to run to keep up.

Inside the tiny, meagerly furnished room, he locked the door, pulled off his sunglasses and threw them on the cheap wood table, then turned to look at her, his blue eyes crinkling into a come-hither smile. "Well, Ms. Marlow."

"Well, Mr. Baxter." She let her coat drop and stood, legs strongly apart, exposed nearly all the way by her tiny skirt, and lifted her chin, daring him to make the next move.

He did. He lunged for her, swung her up and around, tumbled her back onto the bed under him, thrust his leg between hers and kissed her as if he were never going to stop.

Lucy hooked her leg around his and pushed up against him, already so hot she could barely stand waiting for them to undress.

He fumbled with her panties, with his fly, and then he was inside her, fast and hard, saying her name, knowing what she wanted, what she felt, without words even being necessary, making her body crazy exactly the way he knew she liked best, making her heart crazy with how much she loved him.

She started to build to an easy climax already, like in the early days, as if the best parts of both of them were freed from the recent decline, free to express themselves, to find each other again in this cheap little room where her moans were probably easily heard by anyone happening by.

They climaxed together, as if they couldn't bear to be apart even for an orgasm. Lucy wrapped her arms around his broad shoulders, blissful, content, her body coming down to the same slow rhythm as his.

They were meant to be together until death.

Link lifted his head and gazed down at her, quirking his eyebrow. "You are every bit as hot as I imagined you would be."

She giggled. "You're twice."

"Why haven't we been doing this all along? It's incredibly exciting like this." He glanced around and chuckled as if he couldn't believe they were there. "Don't you think?"

"Mmm. Just too bad it was over so soon." She spoke with exaggerated disappointment, knowing he was far from finished.

"You think this is over?" He kissed her and started moving, still hard inside her, then kissed her again, tenderly, sweetly, and pulled back to gaze at her, eyes intense and wide, the way he looked when he was feeling deeply about her. The way he hadn't looked in far too long.

"Lucy, this is just the beginning."

11

KRISTA STOOD AT THE corner of Park and Beacon, the Boston Common green in front of her, the gold-domed State House looming behind her. She shivered slightly in the early-evening breeze, more nervous than cold, totally unsure of what to expect. John Smith's second call had been short and cryptic. No Ritz. No room. Stand at this corner and wait. A car would pull up and she was to get into it.

Gulp. Sounded vaguely Mafia. Would she get fitted for cement shoes in the backseat?

She'd had the presence of mind to ask what kind of car—not that guys drove up and invited her into their vehicles often, but she might as well know. Some faint attempt to feel more in control of the situation. He'd chuckled and said probably not what she expected.

Whatever that meant. So there she stood, trying not to feel like a lamb on its way to slaughter, both physically—though she still felt no real sense of danger from him—and emotionally. Emotionally she was in a great deal of danger.

If she didn't get to see him tonight—

She diverted her thoughts from an ultimatum whose consequences she might not want to accept by imagining what kind of car she'd least expect John Smith to drive.

Not that he'd specifically said he'd be driving it, but who else? Not as though most people had chauffeurs at their disposal, though if he could afford the Ritz, he probably wasn't hurting financially.

Most likely he wouldn't send his wife or girlfriend around for her either. She snorted wryly. Her dream man—a swinger priming her for a threesome.

No way. Possibly she was romanticizing him—doubtless she was—but what had been growing between her and John Smith couldn't be stretched to include anyone else.

So would he pull up in daylight, in the flesh, and dispel the anonymity just like that? Part of her certainly hoped yes. The part that was ready for the next step, ready to see if what she felt for him would only deepen when they emerged from darkness.

Part of her was terrified that seeing him would pop her beautiful fantasy bubble and replace it with the sad truth that John Smith was just another guy. *Guy* meant disappointment and heartache and eventual disillusionment, though she always seemed to get her hopes way up by the time the next one came along.

She really, really didn't want John Smith to turn out to be just another guy. Hell, she'd rather keep seeing him in the dark forever than lose the magic of what they had.

Sort of.

A car pulled up to the curb next to her, an older-model Lincoln Town Car—what she'd expect John Smith's grandfather to drive, definitely not John Smith.

So this was it. She held her breath, unable to see through the tinted windows, aware the driver was male but not able to tell more about him.

The driver-side door opened. A man emerged....

Her breath whooshed out with the release of tension. Not John Smith. This man was quite a bit older and bearded.

"Jane Doe?"

She nodded, feeling ridiculous being called Jane Doe in public, but the driver didn't betray by so much as a smirk that he thought anything was odd about the name or that she was standing there expecting to be picked up by a stranger.

He opened the back door and gestured her in. "Mr. Smith sent me. I'm Frank."

"Thank you, Frank." She slid into the warm comfort of the backseat, stifling an urge to giggle at the thought of being chauffered. If this guy was a friend of John's, he was doing a bang-up chauffeur imitation. If he were a chauffeur of John's, then…well, the Ritz had been her first clue.

She pulled the seat belt over her and buckled it, peering out at a few curious pedestrians watching Frank close her door and move to the driver's seat. Aahh, let them wonder. She grinned and leaned back against the soft padded leather, thinking of Grandma Ellsworth saying it was as easy to fall in love with a rich man as a poor one. Some of her friends also had very, er, *practical* standards for the men they wanted. Money was fine, but Krista had always wanted to fling herself into love for love's sake alone. Just her luck that every time she'd flung herself, her parachute hadn't opened.

Frank shut his door, picked up something from the seat next to him and handed it back to her. An eyeshade. The kind people used for sleeping, to induce total darkness. John Smith's answer to meeting in daylight.

A sharp stab of disappointment. More mystery. More anonymity.

And a tiny warm spread of relief. More mystery. More anonymity.

Maybe this could be a little more confusing?

She put the mask on and leaned back again. Lucy would love seeing her reduced to this mass of conflict. Look at Ms. Black-and-White now. Nothing was straightforward in this situation, nothing concrete and easy to hang on to. She'd undoubtedly judged Lucy too harshly— and, gulp, maybe a few others?

The car pulled away from the curb, an odd sensation to be riding without sight. She must be more of a control freak than she thought, because it was hard to sit and experience turns and shifts in speed without knowing where they were headed or what was in front of them.

Finally after what she'd guess was roughly twenty minutes, the car stopped. Frank got out, opened her door.

"My hand, Miss Doe."

She rolled her eyes at the pompous address and fumbled until she found his hand, hoping a huge crowd of gawkers wasn't gathering to see the masked woman emerge from the chauffeured Lincoln. Out of the car she caught the scent of the sea, heard the squawk of seagulls— were they near the harbor?

Frank's hand moved to her elbow and, feeling incredibly foolish, she followed his instructions to step up, wait, walk forward, until her senses registered the cessation of wind and the impression of being in front of a building.

A jingle indicated Frank had a set of keys to wherever they were. She sensed a door in front of her swinging open; the hand at her elbow urged her forward. Into where?

She held back, throat suddenly dry. "Where are we?"

"Mr. Smith's building."

"His home, right? Not an abandoned warehouse pop-ulated by chain-wielding thugs?"

Frank chuckled. "Not this place. Luxury condos start-ing at three quarters of a million and climbing. Nothing bad ever happens here, they can pay to have it go away. You're safe."

Oh my. Was John Smith's real name Prince Charming? Did he own a small country somewhere? Grandma Ellsworth would be salivating. Krista was, too, but for rea-sons that had nothing to do with money.

"This way."

She followed her escort into the warm building, her heels making echoey taps on the smooth floors. They stopped, waited. If there was anyone else in the hall star-ing at her, she was very glad she couldn't see. Elevator doors opened, they stepped inside. Keys jangled again, and the car started up.

She counted clicks, excitement mounting as they slowed on what must be the fifth floor.

"Here you go." The doors rumbled open. "After you."

She stepped out onto another hard, tappy surface, let-ting Frank guide her into what she sensed was a huge space—a loft?—tap-tapping, then quiet over rugs, then tapping again. All the while her ears were waiting for the sound of his voice or of his movements. Nothing.

Was he here? She was shocked at the depth of her ea-gerness to be with him again. To talk to him, hear him, feel him...and see him?

A door slid back, frigid breeze blew into the warmth. Not exactly cozy patio weather...

Frank led her across a short balcony and placed her hands on a railing. "Wait here."

She nodded and waited, tempted to lift her mask but not wanting to be like women from mythology who screwed up their wonderful destinies by peeking when they weren't supposed to. Pandora, Psyche...

The driver's footsteps receded; the door slid closed, and she was suddenly absolutely sure she was not alone on the balcony.

Shivery excitement—and not just from the wintery temperature.

"Hello, Jane."

She smiled, uncontrollably happy to be with him again. His voice did the same thing his voice always did to her, only more, because he sounded a little tired or dispirited tonight. Along with the usual butterflies, tenderness showed up and a need to make whatever was bothering him go away.

"Hi, John." She wanted to turn around but waited—did he have a mask, too? Or could he see her? The thought left her feeling wide-open and vulnerable. What was he thinking? Was he disappointed in what he saw?

He came up behind her and a comforter came around her shoulders, encasing them so they stood together, cocooned in what was probably down, warm and private in the chilling air.

"Oh, that's nice. Thank you."

"You're welcome." He hugged her back against him. "You can take off your mask."

She stiffened in disbelief. "I can look at you?"

"At the view. I'll stay behind you."

"Gotcha." She fought off the disappointment. Nothing was going to spoil her evening with him. Every time could be the last and she wanted to enjoy every second. "You're not wearing one?"

"No."

So he'd seen her walk in, seen everything but her eyes. This was progress in the direction she'd been hoping progress would be made.

She took off the mask and let out an *oooh* of pure pleasure. The setting sun behind them had turned the light vivid and orange. Boston Harbor glowed dark blue, dotted with islands, ships, buoys and a few smaller craft. "What a fabulous view."

"I thought you'd like it." He watched the scene with her, holding her and the comforter loosely, not seeming in any hurry to continue their erotic journey.

That suited her fine. It felt just right to be standing there with him, as if they were friends or longtime lovers, past the initial frenzy of lust.

As soon as the pleasant thought washed over her, it receded, leaving her insides achy and empty. Friends, longtime lovers, no. John Smith was still a stranger. She wanted to turn around and look, make him look, too, find out who affected her so strongly. But that wasn't part of the deal. At least not yet.

So she stared out at the water instead, past the point where civilization left its mark, where the ocean reached toward the horizon. Gazing at the sea made her restless, as if her tiny existence needed further justification, as if she had too many things left to conquer that she'd never be able to conquer. A bittersweet push/pull feeling, like the waves themselves.

"John?" She spoke without thinking, assuming he'd understand her fairly crazy reaction. Would he? "Does the ocean ever make you feel you're not doing enough, not living enough?"

"Every day."

He got it. Her heart swelled so big her chest tightened. Instinctively she turned to register his expression before his strong arms reminded her not to peek. Though she did get a glimpse of medium-brown hair and found even that tiny bit of identifying information excited her. "Really? You're not just saying that?"

"Really. Now tell me why you asked. What aren't you doing enough of? Is that what went wrong with your week?"

"Sort of." She blew out a breath, vulnerable talking about her passion in a way she'd never been before. "I want to... I'm trying to change the way people think."

He laughed but not cruelly. "Nothing like starting small."

"I know. But I want them to appreciate...natural things. Small things. Things that have real quality, real value. Not to settle for less. We're a consumer society and we have the strongest voice possible in our wallets." She stopped, hoping he wasn't about to glance at his watch and announce he had somewhere to be.

"Don't settle for glitz without substance." He spoke quietly, thoughtfully. "Or support achievement without the talent to back it up."

"Yes. My father does beautiful work at competitive prices, but people flock to the chain print-and-copy shops because they made the buzz, they have the advertising dollars. My mother was passed over for a principal job in favor of someone less qualified who made more me-me-me noise. My sister lost a part in a show to a no-talent airhead bimbo who can barely carry a tune."

She stopped herself before she started sounding possessed. At this point her other boyfriends were generally chuckling, snoring or rooting through her cabinets for snacks. "You probably think I'm hopelessly naive. Or crazy."

"Actually the opposite. You sound very sane to me. And wise. I bet you're not a big fan of Christmas decorations up right after Halloween or commercials that equate product to happiness."

"Yes. Exactly." Her voice went raspy. *Yes, yes, yes.* She cleared her throat and nodded her head toward the sea. "I get tired of people tolerating the ordinariness of everything. I want experiences and food and people and jobs and thoughts to be rare and special, to make the short time we have here a mindful, rich and meaningful experience. Sometimes I feel like I'm shouting into a vacuum, but I have to keep trying."

"I hear you." He squeezed her in a gentle hug. "So what happened this week?"

She watched the wake of a tugboat boil white and fade into navy, trying to form the words. "Did you ever feel passionately about something, possibly to the point of blindness, and then suddenly you get a genuine close-up of another point of view that rings true as well?"

"Rattles you pretty thoroughly."

"No kidding." She breathed in and out, the knot of hurt and confusion starting to untangle and let go. "That was my week."

"It doesn't mean you're wrong in what you believe."

"No." She wasn't wrong. "But maybe too…harsh."

"The world needs passionate people, Jane. Gets the rest of us thinking."

"What are you passionate about?"

"Besides you?"

She glowed. Couldn't help it. If the sky were darker they could pick her up on a satellite view.

"Besides me." She dropped her head back against his

shoulder, still grinning her head off. "What does the ocean make you need to do?"

"Explore." His voice was deep and rumbly next to her ear. "I chose to live close to a view like this to remind me the world is still out there."

"I see." Her grin sickened and died. "It makes you want to go back to your wanderer's life."

"Yes. Bust out of the suit, pick up my backpack and boldly go where no employed corporate executive has time to go. Take in as much of the world and the people and the scenery as I can."

Unfettered by responsibilities…or relationships. "No settling in any one spot?"

"There would always be somewhere I hadn't seen."

Her heart started thumping painfully and she told herself not to care. Finally she was getting a good idea why he'd chosen to keep their relationship anonymous. Not married, not a sociopath, but she'd bet John Smith was a commitmentphobe, in which case their peculiar method of interaction would be tailor-made for him. All the sex, all the excitement and none of the messy relationship issues. What claim could she make on him when she couldn't even initiate contact to set up a date?

Unless she was wrong, her new dream for the two of them was about to get an early wake-up call.

"When you were traveling, when did you decide it was time to move on from one place to another?"

"Interesting question." He held the comforter around them with one hand, trailed the other down her side. "I never thought about it."

"I have a guess."

"Yes?" He pushed under her waistband, left his warm

fingers lying comfortably, possessively, against her bare abdomen.

"I'm guessing it was whenever you started to feel too much at home." She waited for the response, lead weight on her diaphragm making it hard to breathe.

"Hmm." He stroked his thumb up and down her skin. "I'll have to give that some thought."

She smiled tightly. Bingo. Commitmentphobe. Give it some thought? He was a guy. He wouldn't even give it the brain equivalent of a glance.

"What about you? Why does a blind relationship interest you?"

Her smile faded. It didn't anymore. But she couldn't bring herself to blurt it out. "Oh…well, because it's… exciting."

"Because it's anonymous? Because you don't have to risk…getting real?"

An alarm went off in Krista's head. "Did you say 'getting real'?"

"Uh-huh." His mouth came close to her ear; his hand slipped out of her waistband and started exploring her thigh; he sounded completely relaxed and in control. "Shouldn't I have?"

"No, it's just…no. Nothing." She was paranoid. The phrase was common enough.

"So you think it's exciting not to know who I am?"

"Sure." She kept her tone light, rose on tiptoe, arched her back so her rear made contact with his groin. "I think I'll have all my men this way from now on."

His hands stopped moving. "How many more are you planning?"

He sounded so grim, she couldn't help a traitorous

burst of hope. "None. I mean not now. I mean not until... not unless..."

She broke off, feeling like an idiot. She so desperately wanted to mean something special to him, this was almost scarier than when he'd woken her in the middle of the night in Maine.

"Say it." His voice was gentle; his hand tightened on her hip. "Whatever it is. I want to hear it."

God, she so sincerely hoped he did. "Is this...more than sex for you?"

His breath went in slowly. "Logically how can it be? You don't know who I am. You've never even seen me."

Krista frowned. Wasn't that mutual? "You've never seen me either."

"But the back of your head is fabulous."

She laughed briefly, wanting to understand, wanting some idea of where this was going. "You said logically. How about illogically?"

His hand started exploring again; he began a rhythm against her with his hips. "Being with you is more than... more than I expected."

She should leave it alone, she should enjoy the physical and stop pushing. But she needed to know. "More than you want?"

"More than is convenient in some ways, but no, not more than I want. Not anymore." He spoke quietly, gravely, stopped moving against her. "What about you?"

"It's not more than I want either." She whispered the words, tension dissipating in another, more welcome rush of hope. *Right now it's less.*

"What's your idea of the perfect relationship?"

That was easy. Standing watching a beautiful view,

nose freezing, wrapped warmly in a down comforter with the best lover she'd ever had, who'd touched her more deeply in a short time than anyone she'd ever known. "Someone I…am comfortable with, someone I can share anything with, someone who will both listen and hear me. Multiple orgasms wouldn't hurt either."

He laughed. "Can't argue with that. What else?"

"Someone who doesn't care if I put on a pound or two or five or look hideous sometimes."

"You couldn't look hideous."

She half turned. "How would you—"

"Because I have night vision." He answered in a rush, then chuckled awkwardly. "Plus I just saw a third of your profile and it's stunning."

"Night vision?"

"Jane Doe, there is no way you could be anything but beautiful to me."

Krista smiled out at the harbor, hating that his words made her melt, hating that the twilight seemed brighter because of them. She had no idea if they were anything but words, but she loved them.

"Now tell me your idea of the perfect relationship."

"I don't know, Jane Doe." His voice came out low and gravelly. "That's a work in progress."

"Meaning?"

"Meaning my idea of the perfect relationship is changing. Has changed."

"How?" She held absolutely still, as if a giant insect had landed on her and she wasn't sure if it was going to fly away harmlessly or sting the hell out of her.

"I used to think all I needed was a fireplace, a six-pack and twin blondes."

She snorted. "Be still my heart."

"Okay, I wasn't quite that bad."

She squeezed his arm to show she'd been kidding. "And now?"

"Now I think..." He rested his hand against her hip. "Now I think I'd rather have only one blonde, hot and willing."

"From twins to one? That the big change?"

He chuckled. "A hot, willing blonde I can talk to about anything, one who understands what I'm saying, who challenges me to think and motivates me to act and makes me and my life better."

She had to fight to keep from holding her breath. "What made you change?"

"Are you fishing, Jane Doe?"

"Shamelessly."

"Then you know the answer already."

He wrapped his arms around her. She slid her hands along his forearms, loving the feeling of being locked against him, throat nearly closed with emotion, brain open and giddy. "It's the answer I hoped for."

"Close your eyes."

She closed her eyes, turned her head toward him and found his mouth, as she'd expected, feeling tears rise, forcing herself to breathe deeply to keep them at bay while she kissed him.

She was so gone.

He turned her the rest of the way to face him, kissed her over and over, then cradled her head onto his chest, in the curve of his neck.

"Give me another name for you," he murmured. "I never liked Jane Doe."

She hesitated, then dived in. She wanted him to have

at least part of her true identity and see where it went and how it felt.

"Krista." A thrill shot through her at this breach of their still-unspoken rules, double strong when he repeated her name and it sounded sexier and more intimate, new on his tongue, than it would have if he'd used it from the beginning, when he'd first been a stranger.

She rose on tiptoe again, eyes still tightly closed, and offered her lips, pressed herself against him, hard and rhythmic, until the kisses turned wild and needy. He shrugged the comforter higher over them; her pants fastenings gave under his fingers; he pushed the material off her hips and pulled her toward him.

Krista resisted. No. This would be for him. She reached down, found his fly and freed his erection. Then sank into the tent the comforter made around them and took him into her mouth, hard and smooth and hot. Under the down quilt it was dark, safe, anonymous....

Instead of fueling her arousal this time, the thought slowed her movement, made her fingers drop.

This wasn't what she wanted, not anymore. Down here she was giving him pleasure any woman could be giving him. Any mouth, any set of fingers. She was not even a person to him, not a complete being, just pleasure in the darkness.

She let his penis fall from her lips, remained crouched at his feet. As long as they stayed strangers, what they shared emotionally and verbally, no matter how intense, was totally disconnected from their physical relationship.

Two sides, two halves far apart. Like Lucy, living placidly with Link day after day and having to find excitement elsewhere, in another room, in a pretend place.

That wasn't what she wanted. But to take those two

halves and make a whole worth having—and she believed with all her heart it would be worth having—she needed to know who he was.

Would he want that?

"Krista?" He poked his head into the dark, small space. "Is something wrong?"

"Actually...yes."

He squatted next to her, keeping the comforter over them. "What is it?"

"This is just..." She gestured, and her nails made a thin squeak across the soft fabric.

"Not enough anymore."

"No." She whispered the word, leaned forward and, after a few tries, managed to find his mouth, warm and responsive and reassuring...but still in darkness. She pulled back. "We either need to move forward...or stop."

"I agree." He took her shoulders, gently stood with her in their down tent, which now seemed less a haven and more a silly barrier of fear. He fastened his pants at the same time she pulled hers up, both instinctively wanting cover.

Were they dressing because it was over and time for her to leave as anonymously as she'd come? Or—somewhat ludicrously since they'd made love so many times—were they embarrassed to show themselves to each other even partially naked?

The thought was painful, exposing as a mockery the intense closeness they'd shared so far and making her hunger even more for them to start down the road to a true, open, acknowledged connection.

She waited, surprised when he pulled her to him and kissed her, a long, passionate, wonderful kiss that made her eyes close and her arms wrap around him by themselves. Was this goodbye? If so, she wanted to go on saying goodbye forever.

But so much better if the kiss was prelude to a real hello....

The comforter dropped. The world cooled and brightened her eyelids. Her heart pounded. They'd emerged from the darkness. This wasn't the end. This was Chapter One of a new level of their relationship. Of something that had the potential to be the best thing she'd ever known.

John Smith ended the kiss, his last. From now on he'd be kissing her as someone else. Someone real. Someone she couldn't wait to meet.

Krista drew back, took in a long breath, lifted her lids—

And found herself staring into the killer hazel eyes of Aimee's stepbrother, Seth Wellington.

12

SETH WATCHED KRISTA'S expression change from pleasured anticipation, to what he hoped most not to see—the shock of recognition. From there it wasn't too great a leap to expect what would happen next. Dawning suspicion and the promise of anger.

He'd screwed this up, probably from the beginning, certainly at many steps along the way. He never should have stayed in her cabin at the Pine Tree Inn. He shouldn't have contacted her after he got back. He shouldn't have followed up with her after the Ritz. Yes, she was a powerful draw—the most powerful he'd ever experienced. But that didn't justify what amounted to using her.

Today—even before she said it—he'd realized this couldn't go on. Because against all logic and common sense, he was feeling more than lust and affectionate detachment for a woman for the first time since his girlfriend at Skidmore. Based on a few dates? Granted, remarkably intense ones, but he still didn't understand how it had happened so fast and so anonymously. His feelings, and what he suspected might be hers, made it impossible—or at least dishonorable—to continue the charade of pretending he didn't know who she was. His conscience had been kicking him in the butt pretty painfully for a while.

Standing on this freezing balcony, with the universe extending in all directions and the fading sunlight pouring over them, with Krista's blond hair ruffled by the wind and the sight of her smooth skin tempting him, it seemed twice as ridiculous to imagine he'd ever want to go back with her to closed spaces and darkness. Hell, he'd started fantasizing the exact opposite, bringing her with him wherever in the vast world they wanted to go.

The painful irony was that taking this step, freeing them from that blindness, all but guaranteed he'd never see her again. Finally being able to gaze into her beautiful eyes, horrified and accusing as they were, the thought punched him even more painfully than he'd expected.

"You're…Seth Wellington."

"Yes." His voice came out flat, dead, reflecting the way he was starting to feel inside. How had this woman come to matter so much?

"And you…" She took a horrified step away from him; he had to force himself not to reach for her. "You were the guy at the table behind me at Thai Banquet."

"Yes." She remembered that, too. He'd hoped, stupidly, that their first exchange of glances at the restaurant had only had an impact in one direction. The outcome was inevitable now. She'd already begun to piece together a portrait that would be so unflattering he'd barely recognize himself. Certainly it would bear no resemblance to whatever she'd pictured of him so far.

"And you *followed* me? To *Maine?*"

"Yes." What was he supposed to say? He hadn't planned any of this, hadn't cooked up a smooth story, hadn't invented ways to charm her out of her reaction and, for some reason, he didn't have the stomach to try now.

He'd simply realized when she stepped onto the patio tonight—petite and vulnerable with the mask over her eyes and no idea where she was, putting up with all of it just to be with him—that he couldn't keep lying to her.

"That is…it's…it's *creepy*." She was breathing hard now, a touch of fear in her eyes, cheeks reddening from anger and cold.

"Aimee sent her bodyguard after you, to intimidate you. I was chasing him, trying to call him off." He wanted to howl. The explanation was ludicrous.

"Her bodyguard? To intimidate me? This sounds like a bad episode of some daytime drama. Your sister watches too much TV."

He nodded, though he didn't have any idea if Aimee watched too much or any.

"How the hell did she know I was going to Maine? Were you having me watched?"

"I heard you tell your sister."

"You were listening."

"Yes."

"Then…" She took another step back; her face crumpled before she clenched her jaw and set it hard. "You heard me tell Lucy about my fantasy of having sex with a stranger."

Damn it. *Damn* it. "Yes."

"So you followed me to—"

"I told you why I went up there. I was following Juice, her bodyguard, not you. If the hotel hadn't mixed up the keys, you never would have known I was there."

She stared at him as if he was an alien, her fists tight, arms tight, face tighter, and any grab-at-straws hope that she'd appear at all softened by a logical explanation died. "Is this Juice guy big, black leather, beard and a gentle voice?"

The bad feeling in his gut got worse. "You've seen him?"

"He warned me off your sister in the cereal aisle of my supermarket." She crossed her fists over her chest. "Yesterday. Do you have any idea how scary this is getting?"

The sickness rose into his throat. He wanted to punch Juice. And Aimee, too. "She went too far."

"Too far? Further than you planned together?"

"No."

"You've known who I am all along. Was your seduction about keeping me under control?"

He looked her straight in the eye. "The seduction was about wanting you."

She looked startled; her lips parted slightly, and he wanted to kiss her so badly he couldn't believe he had the strength to hold back. He hadn't expected his desire for her to become so much stronger just from seeing her face or the excitement of their interaction to triple every time he looked into her eyes. Nor had he expected the anticipated pain of losing her to rise exponentially.

Did she feel the stronger connection, too, now that she could see him in the light?

As if she sensed the question, the glimmer of pleasure in her eyes died as if a guillotine blade had come down on it. "Was this about making sure I stayed out of the way of the Wellington makeover?"

He shook his head, choked and frustrated. "Not about that."

"I don't like this. I don't like that you lied to me all this time."

"I didn't expect you to like it." His words came out gruffly. Ironic that she'd gotten him talking earlier about escaping it all. He wanted nothing more right now than to escape this ugly and impossible situation.

Except when he got free, he still wanted her with him.

She took in a sharp breath, started a sentence, sputtered, stopped, glared.

He needed to joke her out of this. Give her some perspective. Take her in his arms and kiss her, try to remind her how good they were, what this was really all about.

Why couldn't he? Since when had he been at a loss for words?

He didn't like the answer.

He was scared. The guy who could walk into a strange bar in any small town and make friends with the most hostile local was struck nearly speechless by a fiery, petite blonde he could pick up with one arm.

"Would you have told me who you were eventually if I hadn't brought it up? Or just kept trying to get all the sex you could until I finally figured it out?"

He gritted his teeth at her sarcasm. "It wasn't like that."

"No? What was it like?" She lifted both arms and let them slap down, wind blowing sudden and fierce, as if her anger had called it. "The campaign to soften up Krista so she'll go easier on Aimee and not screw up your new ad campaign?"

"No. I told you. That's not—"

"Is this the latest strategy now, here, tonight? Hint that you have feelings for me, then show yourself so I can't bear to say anything mean about your sister because by now I have most certainly fallen for you the way you planned me to?"

He couldn't help looking incredulous. "God, that's twisted! You think I'm capable of that?"

"How the hell should I know?" She turned and paced three steps away, two steps back, losing ground. "It's pretty obvious I had no idea who you were."

"I know that. But—"

"Come to think of it…" She stopped pacing, stood very still. "I still don't."

"You know me better than most people." Again his voice was flat, tight, matter-of-fact. The fear was so strong, he couldn't even begin to show her how much she mattered.

"Right. Except for the part that counted. That you were using me. A big Wellington laugh riot for all of you."

She tried to push past him and he grabbed her arms, pressure rising in his chest, finally finding a voice. "No laughing. It's been exactly what you thought for me the whole time. The rest of it is details and context. Massively screwed-up details and context, but it's immaterial to what went on between you and me."

"And I should believe you and trust you now why?" Her eyes were intense blue, catching the last ray of the sun, reflecting back into his heart like daggers.

He let her go. "I've given you no reason to trust me."

"Bingo." She walked past him and through the sliding doors into his huge living room.

He lunged after her, her name on his lips, then stopped himself right outside the balcony door. She was going. Damned if he'd beg. Damned if he'd let it show how much this hurt. She had her reasons for thinking he was a jerk. He'd had his reasons for keeping quiet about who he was, and when those reasons didn't hold water anymore, he'd ended the game she'd enjoyed as much as he had.

He had no control over how she felt about it.

He'd just have to let her go.

Over his shoulder the sun disappeared behind buildings, turning the wind bitter. Seth went inside his empty expensive loft and slid the door shut, cutting off air and freshness and light, leaving him in the last place he ever wanted to be again.

Darkness.

13

"So." LUCY SPOKE IN a deliberately false bright tone as she cleared her favorite Parisian Blue dishes from her and Link's extremely late dinner, heart still thudding with giddy excitement after their third erotic adventure at the Cambridge Motel. They'd chatted during dinner in their usual fashion, but the excitement still zinged underneath. She was so thrilled he'd taken to the affair idea and enjoyed it as much as she did. "Did you have fun out with your friends again tonight?"

She finished stacking the plates in the sink and retrieved her red-and-black insulated lunch bag from her briefcase. Same routine, so different now. Instead of dull, robotic resentment, she had a light heart, a smile that wouldn't stop and delicious soreness in a place that hadn't been sore in way too long.

"As a matter of fact, I did." He got up from their Shaker-style kitchen table where he'd been lounging, dropped a kiss on her shoulder and gave a faint wink that had her knees knocking. "Alexis must have made you work *awfully* hard. You got back as late as I did."

"She was a slave driver." Lucy wiped the lunch bag clean and put it on the granite counter to air-dry. "I'm exhausted. I feel like I ran a marathon."

He chuckled and nudged her. "Strangely so do I."

"Hmm. Must be something in the air."

"Must be." He reached to get a clean glass from the cabinet in front of her, and her whole body buzzed with awareness, the way it used to when they were first together. "'Scuse me."

"S'okay." It was more than okay. It was all she could do to keep from turning around, ripping his jeans off and going at it again. She wanted to burst into a song-and-dance number around the kitchen.

The phone rang, a call from Krista, cheating her out of her movie-musical moment.

"Hey, what's up?"

"Oh...stuff."

Lucy's good mood took on an edge of worry. Krista sounded miserable. "Uh-oh. Tell me."

"That guy I was seeing?"

Lucy raised her brows. "You mean not seeing."

"Okay, okay, well, I saw him. Two days ago."

"*Saw* him, saw him?"

"Yes, *saw* him, saw him."

"So what, he looks like an ogre and you're disappointed?"

"No. He looks like Seth Wellington and I'm freaked out."

"You're freaked out because he looks like—"

"Lucy, he *is* Seth Wellington."

"Oh my God." She backed up and met a comforting solid chest behind her. Link drew out a chair from the table and steered her toward it, seated himself on the opposite side and watched, clearly concerned. She mouthed *Krista* and he nodded. "That's unbelievable, Kris."

"Oh, it gets worse. Remember when we were at Thai Banquet, that guy behind us who spilled his water?"

Lucy's smile at Link faded into shock. "Don't even tell me."

"Yup. He was listening to our conversation the whole time. He knew I'd be going to Maine and he knew my fantasy was to be screwed by a stranger."

"Oh, my goodness. That's...I don't even know what it is." She lifted her arm and let it drop back down on the table. "Did you force him to reveal who he was?"

"No. He did it voluntarily after we agreed it was what we wanted."

Lucy frowned harder. Interesting that he'd agreed. The situation sounded pretty complicated. And if she knew her sister, Krista was still trying to paint it black-and-white.

"Why do you think he agreed to show himself?"

"I *thought* it was because he had feelings for me."

"And why don't you think so now?"

"He's Seth Wellington."

"Um, I got that. But it's not an answer."

"He knew who I was the whole time. He took advantage of me."

Lucy drew her brows down. Krista wasn't exactly the victim type. Plus she'd bounded into this gladly, and damn the risks. "From what you told me, the seduction in the cabin was at your instigation. And until this happened, you were giddier and happier to be with this guy than anyone I've ever seen you with."

Link shoved over a napkin on which he'd scribbled *More man trouble?* Lucy nodded and he rolled his eyes and returned to the sink to fill his glass.

"Lucy, none of that was real."

Lucy laughed. "Why do I feel like we've had this conversation before but on opposite sides? Wasn't that what I kept telling you?"

"Yes. But...I thought it could be. I thought...I hoped somehow we could take the excitement and great sex and fantasy and merge it into the reality of our lives."

Lucy nodded, feeling a twinge of dread. Exactly what she and Link still needed to do. They had their fantasy fun...and their real life together. So far the two had stayed way too separate. "So wait, Krista, why can't you do that now? Merge the two?"

"Because he's Seth Wellington."

"I think we've established that."

"Lucy."

"Okay, I'm sorry." Lucy couldn't help a smile. For once Krista was a bigger in-love mess than she was. "He had to know what revealing himself would do to your relationship."

"Maybe he wanted to end it."

"Is that how he acted?"

A sigh. "No."

"Krista..." She grimaced, uncomfortable in the advice-giving role, since their positions were usually switched. "Sounds to me like he wanted to come clean because he cares about you. You keep saying because it's not A, it has to be Z, when there's an entire alphabet of choices in between."

"I've been skewering his stepsister for the last year. How do I know this all hasn't been some weird plot to stop me? I told you about that guy in the supermarket."

"Did you ask Seth about that?"

"Yes." Short silence. "He said his sister sent him. He's her bodyguard."

"And?"

"And so how do I know he's telling the truth?"

Lucy covered the phone to try to muffle a snort of laughter. She didn't mean to be uncaring, but it was so delicious to see her sister wallowing in the same kind of romantic confusion Lucy had spent her last few years.

"What is so funny?"

"Nothing. I'm just so thrilled you finally fell for someone this hard."

"What? Fell for *him?*" She sputtered in outrage. "The guy is a…he's…he lied and he—"

"If you had no feelings for him, you'd shake your head in disgust and move on, like you've done with pretty much every other guy who turned out to be a jerk."

Silence. Lucy winked at Link, drew a heart in the air, patted her chest, then pointed to the phone. He winked back and gave her a thumbs-up.

"Listen, Krista. Before this, did you ever get the sense that anything he told you wasn't true?"

"Well…no. But I—"

"When you found out who he was, did he seem to have a reasonable explanation for everything you hurled at him?"

"How do you know I hurled things at him?"

"Please." Lucy rolled her eyes. "You're my sister. When you're upset and scared, you hurl."

"Scared? What did I have to be scared of?"

Lucy waited a devilish beat before delivering her punch line. "Losing the man you love."

"Oh, pleez. I do *not*—"

"It's okay, don't panic."

"I'm *not* panicking, I'm furious."

"You're terrified. Terrified you'll lose him. Calm down, and when you're calm, think it over. Remember his expressions, everything he said, open your mind, imagine yourself caught in his position and in this bizarre situation you two cooked up for yourselves. Then listen to your heart and it will tell you the truth."

A sob came over the phone and Lucy smiled wider. Her sister was a goner. She'd realize it eventually if she hadn't already. And if there was a God, Seth had fallen just as hard and he'd realize it and then Lucy could be very, very smug for a long time watching her sister as enslaved by passion and love as Lucy had been ever since she met Link.

"Truce?"

"Truce." With a sniffle.

"Honey, Krista, it's going to be okay. Just don't hide behind the fear and the outrage. This is so important. You need to get real."

"God, don't say that." She laughed through tears and hiccuped.

"Call me anytime you need me, okay?" Lucy smiled again. Krista needed her.

"Thanks, Luce. I'm a mess."

"Yup. But you'll get better. I promise."

"You'll be at Mom's Christmas Eve, Saturday?"

"Have I ever missed?"

"No. Of course not. See you then."

"'Bye, Krista." Lucy hung up the phone and got to dance her Broadway number after all.

Link put his glass back on the counter, caught her, spun her around and dipped her daringly low. "I gather the mighty has finally fallen?"

"She has. With a mighty splat." She gazed up into his black-lashed blue eyes and felt that same melting thrill his gaze used to produce. "I just hope this guy cares for her as much as I suspect he does."

He brought her out of the dip and nodded seriously.
"Me, too."

"Really?"

"Yeah." He grinned sheepishly. "She drives me nuts
sometimes being such a know-it-all, but I love her."

"I'm glad." She smiled back at him and started to the
sink to finish the dishes and her nightly chores. "Well, duty
still calls, don't it."

"I'm going to bed." Link yawned and stretched. "Been
a tiring evening. I'm not as young as I used to be."

She barely kept her laughter back. "Could have
fooled me."

"Ha." He circled her waist with his arms. "Forget the
routine. Come to bed with me."

"But I haven't—"

"Shhh." He kissed her neck. "The world won't stop if
you leave a dish or two soaking. Trust me."

"You're sure?" She glanced toward the sink, feigning
deep anxiety at the thought, wishing he'd offer to do it
for her.

"I'm sure." He started walking backward toward the
door, pulling her with him.

"But...but...my dishes!"

He chuckled and swung her firmly around, pushing
her in front of him. "Dishes tomorrow. Bed now."

She relented, giggling, and led the way. Okay, maybe
she'd become too rigid in the last few years. Maybe she
wasn't as much fun as she used to be. Maybe not as spontaneous. Maybe not a big inspiration to the passion she
missed from him? The thought was a huge relief. Something she could work on. Something she could do to make
things better between them, so she could stop feeling so

depressed and helpless. And maybe in time he'd come around, too, help out a bit more, give her the support she missed herself.

All good. Note to self: stop being a tight-ass. Krista should probably learn the same lesson, but maybe that was for Seth to teach her.

She followed Link into their bedroom and changed into her nightgown while he put on his favorite Patriots T-shirt and the plaid boxers she bought him for Christmas years ago. When had they gone to bed at the same time in the last months? Either he stayed up watching a movie or she stayed up brooding. She couldn't wait.

They slipped into the king bed from opposite sides, but instead of going to sleep, she crossed over to him and fit herself to his side, the way they used to, always.

"Today was a good day." She yawned and stroked his solid chest through the soft cotton.

"Amen to that." He chuckled.

"What's so funny?" She adjusted her head on his shoulder, savoring the comforting feel of his strong arm at her back.

"Just remembering a particularly fabulous moment out tonight with the guys."

"I had some pretty great times at work, too."

"Really." He gave her a brief squeeze. "I'm not sure I've ever seen anyone so devoted to her job."

"Mmm." She pressed against him. "I think I'm going to have to work late soon again."

"Yeah, the guys have another date lined up, too."

"Good." She kissed his cheek. "It's important for you to see them as much as possible."

"I agree." He yawned and flung his hand over his forehead the way he did when he was on his way to sleep.

Lucy listened to his breathing, soft and reassuring in the darkness, and felt a wash of love so fierce it was almost frightening. How could she have even thought of putting this at risk with Josh?

"Link?"

"Mmm."

"I think we should go early to my parents on Christmas Eve and help Mom get the roast started. It's harder for her every year."

Silence. Was he asleep? "Link?"

"Lucy...I...wanted to talk to you about that."

Dread. For some reason she felt a landslide of it. "About what?"

"About having Christmas here at home this year. You and me."

She stiffened. Christmas without her family? "But we always go to my parents'."

"I know we always go." Irritation crept into his tone. "I'm suggesting we don't go."

She put her hand to her temple, trying to imagine her and Link here...what, watching TV? "But the decorating and the carols...who will play the piano if I'm not there?"

He sighed. "Never mind, Luce. I just thought it would be a nice change."

"Well, we can be here for New Year's. That's fine. Christmas is...well, it's Christmas."

"Right. Can't argue there."

She lay next to him, wishing there was something more she could say to get them back to their wonderful mood earlier, thinking of nothing. Why wouldn't he want to go to her family's house? Didn't he enjoy being part of it? Why hadn't he ever told her if he didn't?

"Luce?"

"Yes." She found herself bracing for whatever he was about to say.

"Remember our first date senior year?"

She laughed, relief relaxing her. "Like I could forget?"

"Did you ever get the wine stain out of that skirt?"

"Faster than your bruise faded."

"Rocky beginning, huh."

"A little. But considering you asked me to move in with you three months after graduation, I'd say we got past it."

"I'd say." He rubbed her shoulder absently. "Remember the day you moved in?"

"Pouring."

"Of course." He chuckled, then his body tensed and the silence between them felt awkward again. "The first thing you did after we got your stuff in was rearrange all my furniture."

Lucy laughed too loudly, sensing something wrong, not sure what it was. "It was a decorating disaster."

"That bugged me."

She lifted her head and made out his features in the near darkness. He was staring at the ceiling, frowning slightly. She thought back to that day, how excited and nervous she'd been, how strange it had felt to be calling someone else's territory home. How badly she'd needed to put her stamp on the place.

Had she thought about him in all that? How he'd feel having someone move in and turn everything upside down?

No.

"Wow, Link, I...wow. I'm sorry."

"You don't have to be sorry. I don't even know why I brought it up now."

She kept staring at him. Why had he? Tonight? Because he felt close to her? Or because the adventure at the hotel had only underscored how far apart they'd grown at home? Why would he bring something like that up and ruin their perfect day?

"Link. I'm...I—" She stopped, frustrated as hell. Maybe nothing had changed. Maybe she was creating a fantasy no more substantial than Krista's first visit with John Smith in the dark.

"What is it?"

"Nothing." She pressed her lips against his warm stubbled skin, hating that she'd shut him out again but unable to articulate her fears. "I'm glad you told me."

"Really?"

"Yeah. Really."

"So now I can list everything about you that bugs me and you'll be even happier?"

She winced as if he'd hit her, then forced her voice to come out light. "Um...no. But if you want, we can put all the furniture back the way you had it."

"No way. It was a disaster." He found her mouth for a brief kiss. "Good night, Miss Lucy."

He released her and settled himself, partly turned away. She took her cue and moved back to her side of the bed, trying not to be devastated. So they wouldn't make love again and spend the night twined blissfully in each other's arms. That was okay. She'd sleep better this way probably, and so would he. This early in their adventure she couldn't expect miracles.

One step at a time.

She turned restlessly, mounded her down pillow into a more comfortable shape, hearing Link's breathing behind her turn to the deep, regular rhythm of sleep, sure she'd spend most of the night awake again.

Because if a hot, exciting affair with the man she loved didn't work to revitalize their relationship, to bring them back together at home, she didn't know what more she could do.

14

Seth stood on his balcony, gazing out at Boston Harbor, Elvis mug full of hot coffee keeping his hand and his insides warm. The air was heavy and cold and smelled of snow on its way. Christmas Eve.

The grand opening of the stores had been three days earlier. Santas and elves and toy giveaways and special offers and performers and somehow, somehow, he'd pulled it all off. Yes, he'd rather have been able to schedule the opening at the start of the holiday season, but being this close to Christmas had made it special, he had to admit.

It remained to be seen how the new image would affect the stores' bottom line in the future, but the bold splashes of color, the sharp angles and dramatic lighting had produced the perfect effect. Cool but not intimidating, chic but not frighteningly so. Aimee had behaved with great restraint, and even the board members had enjoyed themselves, slapped him on the back and congratulated each other as if they'd been gung-ho from the beginning.

His father had been beside himself with pride and pleasure, emotions Seth was proud and pleased to have been responsible for. Soon enough Dad would jump back in and take over and Seth would be free to move on.

He gazed out at the horizon, waiting for the excited rumblings to start, for the voices of adventure to lure him into fantasies of traveling distances, seeking out new friends and faces and places. But the mighty beckoning ocean only looked aimless and frigid and alone this afternoon. And all that came to him were images of what he'd be leaving behind. Wellington stores. His father. Even Aimee.

And Krista.

A gust of wind whipped across the balcony, sharp and biting, sending him back into his living room, tastefully furnished, tidy and clean as always. Not for the first time he wished Krista had never set foot in the place, that he'd never seen her slender, sweet, iron self in this room. Nearly two years he'd lived in this condo, day in and out, and after one glance of her here, the place seemed permanently cold, empty and ghost-filled.

His apartment bell rang, inducing a burst of adrenaline he immediately tried to suppress. He'd been tempted to call Krista at least fifty times in the last eight days, but what could he say that he hadn't already said?

I love you? He was shaking his head already on his way to the door. He wasn't tough enough to take that kind of rejection.

He hit the intercom button, trying not to hope. "Hello?"

"Seth, it's Aimee. I want to talk to you."

Aimee. What the hell was she doing here? She hadn't set foot in the place since the week after he'd moved in. He only saw her on the rare occasions his father had them both over for dinner. "Is Dad okay?"

"Yes. This is about me."

Seth snorted. Big surprise. He buzzed her in, wearily apprehensive. What this time? She'd landed her own reality TV show, *Aimee Squawks?* She was planning a run for the presidency? She'd decided she was lesbian? Whatever she had to tell him, undoubtedly he'd rather not know.

The elevator doors opened into his foyer and she bounced out and into his living room, bringing fresh heavily perfumed air in with her, bright dark eyes surrounded by too much makeup, dark hair streaked with something glittery gold.

"Hey, Aimee, what brings you here?"

"Oh, just stuff." She took off her hot pink coat trimmed with white faux fur and tossed it onto his couch. "Man, it looks grim in here. Blech. How come you haven't decorated or anything?"

"I've been busy."

"Hey, Scrooge, it's Christmas." She punched his arm playfully, which he hated. "You should deck your halls or whatever."

He gritted his teeth. "What's the news, Aimee?"

"Well, jeez, Seth, I can't just jump into it. I mean, aren't you going to offer me a drink?"

He started to object before it hit him she was old enough. "Okay. What'll you have?"

"Cranberry juice?" She wrinkled her nose hopefully.

He grinned and softened, reached to mess up her hair, which she hated, and went into his kitchen to find the juice.

She followed him, chattering about her latest purchases and the decorating she'd done in her Beacon Hill apartment, upstairs from his father's on Joy Street.

"Ice?" He interrupted, filling her glass with ice without waiting for her answer.

"Sure." She trailed her hand on his scratchless stove and unmarred countertops. "What, you don't ever eat here? Do you even *live* in this place?"

"I'm not much of a cook."

"Well, duh." She watched him pour cranberry juice. "So?"

"So what, Aimee?" He handed her the glass and put his hands on his hips, watching her, feeling the same combination of urges he usually got. To throttle her, hug her or put her in a shower and scrub her into a little girl again. "You're the one with the news."

"Oh, yeah, right. Yeah, well... Dad said he's going to go back to work a year from now, did he tell you that?"

He took in a breath. One more year, then he was free. Was that still what he wanted? So much was changing. "No, he didn't tell me."

"Oops. Well, I'm sure he will soon. He only just kind of mentioned it last night, when we were eating at this fabulous—"

"Is that your news?"

"Um...no." She became suddenly intent on spinning the ice in her drink.

"Spit it out, Aimee." He did not have a good feeling about this. If she was backing out of her contract with Wellington Stores...

"Okay. Well, guess what?" She saw his expression and nodded hastily. "Right. Get to it. Okay, well...I'm getting married!"

Seth groaned silently and sank onto one of his tall kitchen stools, preparing himself to sound happy for her. "Wow. You are? Who's the lucky man?"

"Juice."

"Juice?" Surprise shot him to his feet again. What the hell was this? He wouldn't have pegged Juice for a gold digger. "What is a bodyguard doing proposing to—"

"Oh, well, he didn't really propose to me."

Seth sat again, heavily. "He didn't."

"No." She waved the silly thought away and grinned at him, but warily. "I'm going to propose to *him*. But I'm sure he's going to say yes, I just know he loves me. And then we'll probably—"

"Aimee."

Her grin faded slowly. "Um, yeah?"

He put a hand up to his forehead, closed his eyes. Counted to ten. Twice. Okay. She wanted to get married. That was her business. She was of legal age. He couldn't stand in her way.

But damn it. Married? This went beyond CDs or stage shows or novel writing.

"How long have you been dating?"

"Well *dating* dating, twenty-eight days. That's if you count the first kiss as the official start of the dating period, which I guess you would. But I've known him much longer."

He got off the stool again and started pacing. "What kind of bodyguard gets involved with—"

"Well, that part was sort of my idea, too. Not that he objected or anything."

He narrowed his eyes at her low-cut top and tiny skirt. "I'll bet."

"I know it seems quick, but this is forever love, Seth."

Forever? This from Miss Twenty-First Century Short Attention Span? "And how do you know that?"

She scowled at him as if he was the class dunce. "Well, duh, I just do. That's what everyone says it's like—you just know."

"Like you knew you wanted to be a teacher, a rock star, an astronaut, a—"

"I was a kid then."

"You're a kid now."

"I'm twenty-one."

He took a deep breath. She was right. No point arguing. He should back off and let her make her own messes, learn from her own mistakes.

Except Sheila Bradstone's voice sounded in his head, telling him his sister's actions were a cry for attention. Aimee had come to him before she'd asked Juice. Did she want him to talk her out of it?

For God's sake, that was ridiculous. If she knew it was a bad idea, she could damn well admit it to herself and act accordingly.

His father got in line behind Sheila, telling him he'd always been an observer, afraid of getting his feet dirty.

Then, most painfully, Krista, pointing out that he moved on whenever someplace started to feel like home.

He sighed, poured himself a glass of juice to stall. He could hear Aimee fidgeting behind him. She never could sit still.

No, he wasn't very good at this big-brother stuff. But maybe he needed to try. "You're too young for marriage, Aimee."

"Lots of people get married when they're twenty-one."

"And lots get divorced."

"I know what I'm doing." Her voice was the same pouty brat voice he knew all too well from her phone calls.

Right. His brain yelled at him to back off, stay uninvolved, let her sink her own ship. Then he turned around, caught the tiny plea in her dark young eyes and knew he couldn't, not this time. She'd come all the way here to get help. He wasn't going to let her down again.

He put the glass down, strode out into the living room

and back to his foyer, grabbing her coat from the couch and his from his closet, pressed the elevator button and turned to make sure she'd followed him. "Aimee."

"Yeah?" She'd gone sullen, defensive, arms crossed tightly over her chest. "What?"

"It's Christmas Eve." He grinned and threw her the ghastly pink coat. "Let's go shopping."

"Shopping?" Her mouth dropped open. "You want to go shopping? With *me?*"

"Sure. I have some presents to get. What do you want for Christmas?"

"I thought your secretary did that." She eyed him suspiciously, but he thought he caught a gleam of genuine pleasure.

"Not this year. I also want to talk to you about this marriage thing. I don't think it's a good idea yet. Wait until you know yourself better. And while we're at it, you need to think about college, studying English or Creative Writing so you can write a really good book you can be proud of."

She stood frozen, her lower lip pushed out in a pout. Seth sighed. Maybe he wasn't up for this job.

Tears gathered in her eyes, proving the pout to be the genuine article.

"What's the matter?" He braced himself for another hissy fit, though this felt different and he wasn't sure why.

"I don't know." She wiped the tears, smudging all the god-awful gunk she had around her eyes, making her look younger and vulnerable, like a girl who'd been experimenting with her mom's makeup. "When you talk that way, you sound like a father."

"Like Dad?"

"No, like a TV father. You know, like you give a flying

freak. Whatever." She shrugged, the pout turning who-cares again, and pretended fascination with getting her ugly coat zipped.

"I do care." And no one was more surprised than he was by that pronouncement turning out to be true. "You're my sister."

"Aw, jeez, Seth." More tears. She looked in horror at her black smudgy fingertips. "You're making me run my mascara."

"No!" He clutched his throat and made a gargling sound. "A fate worse than death."

She rolled her eyes at him and flounced to the elevator.

He followed, grinning, mind whirling. Instead of backing off, he'd gotten involved, and tentative as it was, Aimee had responded.

Interesting. He followed her extreme pinkness onto his elevator and pushed the button for the first floor. "All aboard for Wellington's."

A plan started forming for after his shopping trip with Aimee—if he survived. Once he'd talked more to her about applying to college and putting off her marriage proposal, he was going to make a phone call and see if he could talk himself into getting even more involved.

This time with Krista.

LINK POKED HIS HEAD into their kitchen, dressed in his holiday outfit of dark pants and necktie and the red sweater Lucy bought him a few years back, jingling his keys impatiently. "Ready?"

Lucy looked around at the table covered with cookies she had yet to pack into tins and bit back the obvious reply, *Does it look like I'm ready?* "Not yet."

Christmas Eve afternoon and the whole day so far had been horrible. Link was edgy and irritable and her nerves were shot. Obviously once he'd admitted he didn't want to go to her parents', he'd stopped bothering to pretend he did.

"Want some help?" He jingled the keys again until she wanted to rip them out of his hand and throw them out the window.

"No, thanks, I can handle it."

He glanced at the kitchen clock. "I thought you wanted to leave at one."

She stiffened. Okay, so she was late, why not rub it in a little more? "I *did* want to leave at one, I got behind, *okay?*"

"Well, if you're behind, Lucy Marlow, why the hell don't you let me *help?*" He strode to the table and picked up a frosted gingerbread Santa, brandished it in the air between them as if he was giving her the finger. "I'm so useless I can't even pack cookies? All I'm good for is an occasional fuck in a hotel room, is that it? This is bullshit, Lucy."

She stepped back from the table as if he'd slapped her. Oh my God. *Oh my God.* "I can't believe you said that."

He closed his eyes wearily, tossed the cookie back on the table, where it broke in half. "I can't either. I'm sorry. I just wish we were staying home and it made me grumpy."

"No. I mean…" She swallowed, feeling herself starting to shake. She made him feel useless? "Link, I didn't realize you felt that way. Why didn't you tell me?"

"I don't feel that way." He glanced at her balefully. "Much. I tried to tell you. Maybe it wasn't the right way. I'm no good with that stuff, you know that. I need to try harder."

She dragged a chair out from the table and sank into it.

"I rearranged your furniture. That's what you were trying to tell me. That's why you brought that up."

"Luce." He dragged his fingers through his carefully combed hair and messed it up into looking like him again. "Look, I'm sorry. Why don't I help you pack the cookies and we can go to your parents' and forget it."

"No." She shook her head, got to her feet, walked over to where he stood and gazed up at him, feeling as if she was in the middle of a surreal dream. How many times had she done this? Taken over, refused his help and then resented him for it? "We can't forget this."

"What do you mean?" His jaw set; fear invaded his eyes. "Lucy..."

"Watch." She turned from him, went over to the phone and dialed her parents. Their problems weren't going to be fixed by sex in a hotel. The solution had to come from inside their home, inside them. And now by the grace of God—or Link—she thought she finally understood her share of messing up this relationship. And this was her first symbolic step in the right direction.

Her mom answered in the cheerful hello that always sounded like the opening notes to a song.

"It's Lucy."

"Hey, Lucy." Her mom's voice turned wary. She knew her daughter inside out. "Merry Christmas Eve."

"Mom." Lucy turned away from Link, who stood as if he were waiting for the executioner's blade. "I'm sorry this is so last-minute. Link and I want to spend Christmas Eve here at home this year."

"Is there a problem? Are you two all right? You're not pregnant, are you?"

"No." She glanced back at Link, still in the doorway,

clearly stunned. "We're fine. I'm not pregnant. We need… time for us this year."

"Oh. Well…I understand." Her mother still sounded anxious. "If you're sure nothing's wrong."

"Nothing's wrong." Lucy closed her eyes, smiling. In fact, everything was about to be right. "I'm sorry it's so last-minute."

"Sweetheart, it's okay." Mom's voice was back to cheerful. "Link comes first. You tell him I know he loves us, but he's a darn good actor and he put up with us superbly for the last six years. It's about time you let him off the hook."

Lucy blinked. Her mom knew Link didn't enjoy going? And she didn't? How long had the obvious been whapping her on the head while she'd been off in her own world?

"Thanks, Mom. We'll be there tomorrow. After lunch?" She looked questioningly at Link, who nodded, gazing at her as if she was someone brand-new and wonderful, and oh please, she hoped she could be.

"Okay, darling girl, Merry Christmas. We'll see you tomorrow."

Lucy moved closer to the wall and lowered her voice. "You sure this is okay, Mom? I feel like a rat for—"

"What, you don't think we can survive without you? Did I raise you to be that self-centered?"

Lucy started, then laughed uncomfortably. "Of course not, Mom. And thanks."

"Think nothing of it. If Krista has friends she'd rather see, maybe I'll take your father out somewhere and give myself the night off. Change of tradition for all of us."

Lucy's matchmaker brain kicked into gear. "Mom, she'll kill me if she knows I blabbed, but I think there's someone she'd really like to spend tonight with."

"Really?" Her mom sighed. "Mothers are always last to know. Have fun, sweetheart."

"I will." She hung up the phone and turned back to Link, smiling hopefully, desperately wanting this to be the best Christmas Eve they'd ever spent together.

"Luce, it's your family, the traditions—you've gone every year." His protests were no doubt genuine, but his eyes were thanking her from the bottom of his heart.

"Well, I'm not going this year. We can start our own traditions. Like…" She threw out her hands to him. "Well, tell me what *you'd* like to do."

"Watch TV?" He gave a sexy grin to show he was teasing and she giggled.

"We have almost nothing to eat…peanut butter, hot dogs…cookies by the million." She opened the refrigerator, bent forward to check the lower shelves and frowned. "Is the Stop & Shop open? We can get a tiny roast or maybe a Cornish hen, some brussels sprouts—you like those. Or—"

Hands landed on her hips, pulled her back until she was in contact with a very male pelvis that turned her thoughts far away from food. How long had it been since they'd made love here in their own home? And her first impulse had been to organize the same type of feast she'd have at her parents' house?

"Lucy."

She let the refrigerator door swing shut. "I'm thinking peanut butter, hot dogs and cookies will make a great Christmas Eve dinner."

He turned her, lifted her into his arms and strode down the hall. "I agree."

In their bedroom, he fell with her onto the bed and laid his hand on her stomach, eyes searching hers, blue and serious, dearer than her own life. "I have something I want to tell you."

She swallowed, praying it was something good. "What is it?"

"Lucy." His brows drew down, face went tense. "I've been cheating on you."

Relief poured through her. She put on a horrified face. "No! It can't be! Say it's not so!"

He kept back a smile. "This hot babe propositioned me online. I've been meeting her at the Cambridge Motel for wild, incredible, amazing sex."

"Oh my God!" Lucy choked back a giggle. "How could you?"

"I'm sorry. But it's over." He bent and kissed her gently. "It was a big mistake."

Her giggles died. "Why do you say that?"

"She wasn't what I wanted. You are. She was a fantasy. A damn good one. But what I want is you in this bed, right here, for the rest of my life."

Lucy took in a long breath and closed her eyes. There was not a single other combination of words that could have been more perfect to hear. His lips touched hers, he kissed her again and again, until kisses weren't enough and she felt his impatience for her rising.

"Link. I have something to confess, too."

"Mmm?" He went to work on her neck, slow, sensual kisses, then started unbuttoning her red silk blouse. "Make it quick."

"I was cheating, too. I—" Link nipped her and she squealed. "Okay, never mind."

He chuckled and helped her out of her clothes before she helped him out of his. They made slow, passionate love, indulging each other's bodies, whispering all of Lucy's favorite gooey words, together as they should be, as they hadn't been in far too long.

Afterward she lay sated, content, relaxed, welcoming the warm weight of him on top of her, welcoming this chance to change traditions, to make their own and move on together.

"Link."

"Mmm."

"I think this beats the hell out of caroling and tree trimming."

"Seriously? I dunno...I *really* miss that sherry." He laughed when she smacked him. "It's a fine time, Lucy. I just wanted you here with me this year...and speaking of which, you want to do presents now?"

"Now? *Before* din—" She caught herself and clapped her hand over her mouth. "God, have I always been this bad?"

"Yup." He kissed her and moved to the edge of the bed. "But I love you anyway, Lucy Marlow."

"No kidding?" She drew her hand down the bumpy ridge of his spine, wanting to lie with him, wondering why he was suddenly so into presents. "Coincidentally I love you, too, Link Baxter."

"Yeah? So where's my present?"

She rolled her eyes and got up to forage in their closet for the gift she'd gotten him, wrapped in a plain business envelope and a ribbon.

He thanked her with a kiss, tore it open, stared in disbelief, then up at her as if she'd lost her mind but he couldn't love her more even without it. "A membership to a mail video service? You *want* me to watch more movies?"

"I want you to do what makes you happy. And I want

to watch them with you, too." She made a face. "Uh… some of them."

He laughed and pulled her in for a long, grateful hug. "Thank you, Lucy. This means a lot more to me than what it is, if that makes any sense."

She nodded and traced the strong, straight line of his collarbone with a shaky finger. "I'm sorry retroactively for all the times I—"

"Shh. None of that. We've both messed up. We're looking forward now." He put his finger on her lips. "I'll show you what I mean. You ready for my present?"

"Yes. I'm ready." She laughed for no reason but happiness, heart way full of love, feeling as if the world was nothing but endless possibilities again. For the two of them.

He leaned over and rummaged under the mattress. "It's something I should have given you a long time ago."

She flinched comically. "The boot?"

"About as opposite from that as you can get." He straightened and handed her a black velvet jeweler's box.

Lucy stared at it, then up at him, tears wasting no time springing into her eyes. A ring. Marriage. This was why he wanted to be home for Christmas Eve—and she almost didn't let him. How many other times had she stood in the way of her own happiness and his?

Still he loved her, flaws and all, open and accepting. That was a real gift, one that truly humbled her.

"A lot of things have changed since we first met, Lucy. A lot of things. We've grown up and done most of that growing together. We've also managed to iron out some speed bumps along the way, a lot of them in the past few weeks."

The tears started dripping off Lucy's chin. She clutched the box, hardly daring to open it.

"But one thing has never changed." His voice deepened, grew husky. He got off the bed and knelt next to it, wearing only a smile and a look of absolute adoration. "I love you, Lucy Marlow. Marry me, be my wife, stay with me forever."

"I will." She stared at him, nearly sobbing, and hiccuped. "Yes."

He climbed back on the bed for an endless wet, salty kiss, then drew back and tapped the black velvet lid. "So open it."

She opened the box and blinked at the stunning pearcut diamond, sparkling and wavering through her tears. "It's beautiful, Link. When did you get it?"

"You won't believe me." He grinned wickedly. "The day you asked me to cheat with you."

"Why then?"

"Before that, we were on a slow boat to disaster. More like roommates than lovers. I thought you were having an affair with that guy at work."

"Josh? God no, that was—"

"I know what it was now. Back then, I didn't. But when you wanted me in a hotel, it was such a crazy, desperate idea, I knew he was nothing. I knew you still cared, that you still wanted us to work out." He took the ring, slid it reverently onto her finger and squeezed her hand. "And I knew that we would."

"I knew we would, too." She gazed rapturously and reached for him; he wrapped her in his arms.

"Will you marry me soon, Luce? In January?"

"Yes, of course." She touched his cheek, stroked his beautiful male jaw, unable to believe how far they'd come in such a short time, after so many months fearing they were doomed, knowing they'd keep the path they'd cleared to each other open from now on. "And when we have a baby and need space for a nursery?"

"Mmm?" To his credit he got only slightly pop-eyed with terror.

Lucy grinned and poked him in the shoulder. "I'm going to let *you* rearrange all the furniture."

Christmas Eve

WHAT IS REAL?

How can you tell?

Say you spend the night with someone and the sex is perfect and the conversation is perfect and it's everything you've ever wanted. The next morning you wake up and realize you don't know this person at all. And you're faced with the fact that all that powerful magic, all that passion, that deep connection, is based only on your fantasy of who you wanted that person to be.

What if you tell yourself to get real, but the morning after feels less real than the night before?

Then what?

What if Aimee Wellington's book is a bestseller and makes a lot of people genuinely happy?

What if we all admit that Yum-Kake brand Chocolate Kreme KupKakes don't taste anything like chocolate or cream, but we like them anyway?

All things and all people should come with labels. One hundred percent artificial ingredients. One hundred percent real. Fifty percent artificial ingredients but with pleasurable benefits outweighing the detriments. Ninety-nine-point-nine percent bullshit.

Who can be the Get Real labeler? I thought it was me. Now I'm not so sure. I'll be on vacation for a couple of weeks. Maybe some of you will have answers for me when I get back. Merry Christmas.

Krista gazed mournfully at her blog post. Her readers would be furious. People expected her to know, to care, to take a stand, to spare no sarcasm where sarcasm was due.

Right now it was due at herself.

Krista Marlow seemed to think that having sex in the dark with a hunky guy made for a pretty good fantasy. She even imagined that she'd fallen in love. When exactly did she expect to Get Real herself? How was she different than Aimee Wellington, launching herself headfirst into whatever came up without stopping to check it out or think it through or at very least make sure she knew what she was doing?

Worse, once she got real, once she realized what a fool she'd made out of herself, she still couldn't stop wanting him back—correction, wanting the fantasy of him back. Theoretically all she had to do was find someone else and transfer the excitement, the newness, the thrill of being desired, to a man she could be Krista Marlow with from the beginning, not Jane Doe.

Except she *had* been Krista Marlow from the beginning with Seth, not just because he'd known her identity. He'd wanted to know more about her, to understand more about her than anyone she'd ever been with, and she'd given him nothing but herself from that first night in the cabin. Most men just wanted you to know about them. And the testosterone surge at the beginning of a relationship made them pump themselves up to ridiculous lengths. Bragging about sexploits, bragging about physical prowess, intelligence, accomplishments...penis length if nothing else.

But John—Seth—hadn't postured, hadn't bragged. The sick irony of the situation was that unless her instinct for recognizing sincerity had misfired, he hadn't attempted to conceal a single aspect of himself...except who he was.

So did that make what they'd shared more real? Or, given who he turned out to be and his probable motives for gaining her favor, less?

She didn't know. She'd mulled the situation over and over in her head for the last week and a day until she was ready to scream. She'd turned in the holiday-getaway article to *Budget Travel* magazine, the article about cereal and the proposal for a "cranky consumer" column to *Woman's Week* magazine. Submitted a quirky, fun piece asking a big *Why?* of people who fell madly in love with movie stars to *Today's Girl*.

Since then she'd been trying to come up with other ideas, casting her mind for anything that seemed a likely topic for a diatribe. Tanning salons, hair dye, plastic surgery. People wanting to look like anything but what they actually looked like. Why not just accept that nature made you the way you are?

But she worked out regularly—wasn't that her way of not gaining the weight she'd gain if she ate as much as she naturally did? She'd spent thousands having the hair on her legs permanently removed—no more shaving, hurray! But wasn't that artifice of a different kind? Was she the pot calling the kettle black? The resident of a glass house hefting a stone?

Stagnation.

She'd turned in the review of a new play the day before and her editor had told her the full-time staff position would definitely open up in the new year, when the current reviewer retired. For the first time she'd actually been interested. Excited at the thought of steady work, of building a career in one place, tired of the scattered life. Maybe she'd been a slightly altered version of Seth's wandering man, but she was ready to settle down. Now she had to find some way to adjust her dream of settling down to exclude him.

After their Romeo and Juliet balcony scene had deteriorated to Lord and Lady Macbeth, she'd been on fire with the outrage of betrayal. Seth Wellington was wrong, untrustworthy, manipulative. Krista Marlow right, used, the victim.

Clear as crystal—until the crystal shattered and sliced her with the pain of missing him. The phone conversation with Lucy, who'd practically taken Seth's side, had only confused her more. What would she have done in his shoes? Would she have clung to the darkness any less tenaciously? What if his feelings had grown to feel as real as hers did?

The phone rang and she roused herself from her computer-chair brooding and reached for the receiver, trying not to think about it being Seth, because it wouldn't be, so get over it already.

"Hey, merry Christmas Eve." Lucy's cheery voice made Krista want to cry.

"Hey, Luce."

"Uh-oh. No holiday spirit?"

"I'm just...tired. Had a nap. I'm about to head to Mom's."

"That's why I'm calling. Link and I aren't going."

"You're not?" Krista pushed out of her chair. She'd missed the Christmas Eve family event a few times, but never Lucy. "Are you okay? Is everything okay?"

"I'll say." Lucy laughed giddily. "We're having a private celebration."

"He bought you a *ring!*" The last word came out on a shriek.

"Yes, can you believe it? We're getting married next month."

"Next month!" Krista squealed. "Lucy, that's fabulous! Amazing!"

"See what hotel sex can do? I bet you're next with Seth."

"Right." Krista's smile faded. She went to the window, saw couples and families strolling happily down the garlanded beauty of Charles Street as if they were posing for photo ops. She wanted to stick out her tongue.

"You haven't called him, have you."

"Lucy…"

"Mom and Dad want to go out tonight since Link and I won't be there. I gave them our present early and got them a last-minute reservation at the Copley. Either you go with them and play third wheel or pick up the phone and try for what you really want."

Right. Just like that. "It's not that easy, Lucy. I don't even know which man I fell for or why or—"

Lucy guffawed. "Listen to you! Guess what, Krista! It *is* that easy. Black-and-white, just the way you like it. What felt real? Deep down, where it counts?"

Krista closed out the Norman Rockwell scene outside and thought about her time with John Smith. Deep down? She'd sensed from their first meeting he wasn't a lunatic or a danger to her physically. At the Ritz she'd finally cleared her mind to a place that felt more real, more the essence of who she was than anything she'd ever felt before. And in that very clear place, he'd been with her. On the balcony she felt he understood her and her passions better than anyone ever had.

Was that love when you could connect that completely to another person?

"It felt real with him." Her voice came out a terrified whisper.

"Exactly. Don't you dare stand in your own way or I'm coming over there to kick some wimpy Krista butt."

Krista listened to her sister, newly confident, strong, clear about what she wanted—but then, she'd always been clear about Link. Even when their relationship seemed to have all but crumbled into hopelessness.

Was it that easy? Pick up the phone, hi, hello, how are you, let's find out what this means?

Her eyes opened. Signs of life flowed through her veins for the first time in days. Except... "It's Christmas Eve. What are the odds he'll even be free?"

Lucy groaned. "Krista, you don't know the first thing about love. Trust me. If you call wanting to see him, he'll be free. Now go do it. I'm calling back in two minutes, and if the phone isn't busy, I'm calling him for you."

"You wouldn't."

"Would, too."

"No way."

"Truce, Krista." She laughed. "And good luck, sweetheart."

"Truce. Merry Christmas. And congratulations, Lucy. To Link also."

She hung up the phone, flushed, nervous as hell, and

let out a stupid giggle of fear and excitement. It wasn't this simple. It couldn't be this simple.

She dialed his number, pacing forward, hung up on the first ring. Dialed again, pacing back, made it to two rings, hung up again. Dialed a third time standing by the window looking out at Christmas.

This time she put the receiver to her ear and waited.

15

KRISTA STOOD OUTSIDE Seth Wellington's extremely luxurious harborside condo building, shivering. Yes, it was cold; big, fat, peaceful flakes of snow had started drifting down from the heavens like God's perfect Christmas decoration. But most of her trembling had nothing to do with the temperature or the beauty of the evening or the occasion of Christmas Eve.

Seth hadn't answered when she called earlier—she'd had to leave a nervous message on his machine—but he'd called her back twenty minutes later. She'd picked up the phone, sure it was him, and his voice, deep, resonant and familiar coming over the line, had sent up such violent waves of longing she'd feared capsizing completely.

"Krista?" The same voice came over the intercom now, crackly, distorted but him.

"Yes." Her shivering increased even after the buzz sounded and she pushed into the warm, silent building, all marble and columns, decorated for the season with gold urns of greenery, white frosted branches and stems of red berries.

The elevator waited; she walked on, heels clicking too loudly, clutching the silly but appropriate present she'd bought on the way over, not wanting to show up empty-handed on Christmas Eve.

This was the right thing, coming over tonight. If Krista

had decided to spend the evening out with her parents, she'd be climbing the walls. One way or the other, she needed to resolve these feelings—though, of course, she preferred one way to the other by about a million to one.

The elevator arrived at the fifth floor. Krista blew out a nervous breath and pasted on a polite smile, having no idea how she'd respond to him when the doors rolled open.

Though since they were rolling open now, she was about to find out.

He stood in the foyer, tall, handsome, sexy as hell in black pants and a white shirt with green and gray that caught the hazel hues in his eyes. Sexy as hell...but a stranger. A man she'd seen on television, son of a man who'd taken his parents' modest business and turned it into a booming success.

"Merry Christmas." He looked serious, slightly apprehensive, as if he didn't know whether to take her in his arms, shake her hand or bring up a protective force field.

Maybe all of the above.

"Merry Christmas." She took an awkward step out of the elevator, feeling like a teenager on a blind date.

"Come in." He gestured her into the familiar space, the elegant gray and black and burgundy softened and warmed by a Christmas tree and a fire burning in the fireplace.

"You decorated."

"Aimee insisted." He looked around as if the view surprised him. "I'm glad she did. It's a nice touch."

"Definitely." She walked into the room and stood clutching the box she'd brought him, pretending to admire the decorations, wondering how she was going to live through the strain of the evening.

"Can I take your coat?" He came right up behind her, standing too close, hands laid on her shoulders, and suddenly he was John Smith again, and she closed her eyes, went into hormonal overdrive, wanting to lean back against him, feel his hands on her, his body—

"Krista?"

"What?"

"Your coat?"

"Oh. Yes." She had to clear her throat and put the present on his glass coffee table. "Thank you."

She lowered her shoulders; he took the coat off and she heard the swish of the material landing on a sofa or chair.

He didn't move away. "Turn around."

She turned reluctantly, dreading the expected jolt of recognition combined with a corresponding jolt of non-recognition.

"Look at me."

She looked into his eyes, trying to see the person she'd imagined he'd be and, of course, failing.

"I want us to try again." His gaze held hers earnestly. "If you agree, I want to start over, either as strangers—"

"We are strangers."

"Only by sight."

She lowered her head, studied the narrow line of her pointy-toed shiny black shoes on his Oriental rugs. He'd never seen her feet. They'd been beyond intimate several times and he had no idea what her body looked like.

"Either as strangers or...?" she prompted.

"Or as lovers." The deep voice just over her head made her look up. Looking up made her see Seth Wellington.

She didn't want to see Seth Wellington. She wanted to see John Smith. She didn't even know what John Smith looked like, because John Smith wasn't real...which didn't seem to stop her wanting him.

Oh crap.

She was a basket case.

"Do you need time to think about it?"

"Maybe that's a good idea."

"Okay."

She expected him to step back, give her room, literally as well as figuratively. Instead he tipped her chin up and caught her lips in a surprise kiss. She closed her eyes—the better not to see you with, my dear—and *then,* oh, she couldn't help kissing him back, feeling the familiar, smelling his scent, touching the tantalizing firmness of his body.

He hauled her closer, kissed her as if she belonged to him, wrapped his arms tightly around her so she couldn't escape if she wanted to.

She didn't want to. Her eyes stayed closed, arousal burned, she moaned in her throat, rose on tiptoes to press against him.

"I missed you, Krista." He whispered into her temple, kissed a path back to her mouth. The sound of her real name on his lips was wonderful. The feel of his hands running over her hips under the thin rayon of her pants even more so.

She kept her eyes screwed shut, slipped her hands under his shirt, explored the warm landscape of his back, so familiar here in the darkness. "I missed you, too, um…"

Damn. She couldn't even call him that other name.

He pulled his hand out from under her waistband, moved back, staying silent until she opened her eyes and found him watching her, one eyebrow quirked up in an expression she should be familiar with.

"It's Seth, Krista."

"I know." She found her shoes fascinating again. "I'm…sorry. I don't know if this is going to work."

He was silent again. She abandoned her shoes and found him smiling. He had a wide, disarming smile. She tried to imagine it back into the darkness all the times she knew he'd been smiling.

"What's so funny?"

"It's going to work, Krista. We were just rushing things a little. I admit I find it pretty hard to stay away from you." He held out his hand with another of those killer smiles that yes, okay, could make a girl a little crazy. "Come with me."

She snatched up the present from the coffee table, not even sure why—maybe it felt like some kind of symbolic defense held tightly to her chest—and followed him across the room, up a curving wooden staircase with a beautiful wrought-iron railing, up to the loft where his bedroom must be.

At the closed doorway, she hesitated. "Is more sex going to cure what's wrong between us?"

He grinned. "I certainly hope so."

"I'm not sure that's—"

"Trust me." He pushed her hair back on both sides of her face, rested his forearms on her shoulders. "I think you already do or you wouldn't be here, am I right?"

She nodded and gave him a wry smile. "I trust you. I'm not real happy about it, but yes, I do."

He chuckled, opened the door and pulled her through into his bedroom…and into darkness. Again.

"Are we…what is this going to…if we keep—"

"Shhhh." He was there in front of her, a towering warmth, John Smith, leading her, unresisting, over to his bed, gently pulling her onto it, lying next to her, a solid familiar-again presence. She put a hand to his chest, feeling his heart beating through the soft material of his shirt, hating the weakness that made him so irresistible to her this way.

But how would this solve anything? "So we're going to be mole people from now on? That's the solution?"

He laughed and she couldn't help joining him in a nervous giggle. "I have a plan and it's not about mole people. Okay?"

She swallowed. "Okay."

He got up from the bed and went over to the wall. Seconds later a soft jazzy tune started playing, "I'm Dreaming of a White Christmas."

"Mmm, that's nice." She lay back, ready for whatever he had in mind.

She didn't have to wait long. His weight burdened the mattress next to her; her red sweater slowly lifted up and off. "About time I got to see what you were wearing before I took it off you."

Krista laughed and fumbled for his shirt buttons, feeling giddy until it hit her. Giddy to be in fantasyland again? What was she doing? This could make everything worse.

And yet…right now it was making everything so much better.

He kissed her exposed skin—nearly unerring in guessing where it was—then lowered her pants and took his time removing them from each leg. She returned the favor with his, admittedly enjoying the feel of the material all the more for being able to picture it on him earlier.

Half-naked, her body heating, when she most expected the next step, he was gone, down at the foot of the bed doing…something.

A scraping sound, the flare of a match dwindling to a soft, dim glow—a candle?

He came back on the bed, a barely illuminated silhouette. She could see his hands now, dark shapes moving across her skin, slowly removing her bra and panties. In turn, she could just see to find his boxers, pull them down his long, shadowy legs, make sure they landed well away from the tiny light at the foot of the bed.

Then he was gone again, another match, a slightly stronger glow. This time she could barely make out his features, the strong nose and jaw, the darker line of his brows.

She closed her eyes as he kissed her but opened them again when he moved down to her breasts, straining to see the outline of his lips on her nipple. Her body immediately knew he was no stranger—arousal flooded her, warm and welcome as his touch on her skin.

Another candle lit, his mouth moved between her legs. Again she closed her eyes; again she had to look, fascinated by his face slowly coming into sharper relief. His nose had a slight bump halfway down, his forehead was broad and smooth, his hair thick and with a slight wave.

Then his tongue began to work and she felt herself moving up to the next level of desire. Her head fell back, she stared at the shadows flickering on the ceiling, let out a soft moan when the sensations became too much for feeling and had to be translated into sound.

He moved away again. The room brightened. He returned to her, this time holding a condom. *Not yet.* She pushed him back on the bed and knelt, studying him. His feet were wide and callused, the hair on his legs curled and light, the muscles in his thighs tight and long. A dark freckle graced one pelvic bone; his erection stood tall from its nest of hair.

She closed her mouth over that erection, watching him, unable to stop. He gave the sigh she'd heard so many times in the dark, eyes closed in bliss, mouth slightly open. She sucked and watched, learned from his expression how to please him best.

Then he pulled her up next to him...and left to light one

more candle, bringing the room to soft twilight—or maybe dawn. He put on the condom and lay next to her again, arms around her, stroking her, memorizing her body with his eyes.

Seth Wellington IV. He had a tiny white scar marring the perfect shape of his lower lip. He'd missed a place shaving near the corner of his mouth; the bristles were slightly longer there. One sideburn had been cut slightly shorter than the other.

He moved over her, and when their eyes met, his were lit warm and tender, and she welcomed him into her body, wondering how she could ever have made love to him before without being able to see the way he felt about her.

Seth Wellington IV.

He pushed inside, in and out, slowly, beautifully, reverently, gradually building faster until they both climaxed, Krista first, Seth soon after, looking into each other's eyes in awe, finally able to see what they'd been experiencing all along.

After, she touched his face, touched the smooth forehead, his fine cheekbones, narrow, fine lips. "Seth."

He smiled.

She touched the crinkles at the corners of his eyes. "Thank you."

"For?"

"What you did. With the candles. It was perfect. It helped me…merge you with…him." She gestured helplessly, thinking how strange she'd ever resisted.

"You have no idea how glad I am." He rolled to his side pulling her onto hers so they were facing each other in the warm glow of the candles. "This last week without you has been hell."

She nodded, noticing for the first time his bangs curled

over to conceal a widow's peak. She touched it, too, greedy for every physical detail. "Hell for me also."

"Aimee told me my father intends to come out of retirement a year from now, January first. After that I will no longer be running Wellington Stores."

"Oh." She felt her heart wanting to retreat to safety. Out of his corporate job, he'd go wandering. Wouldn't he? Tears threatened and she sat up quickly, unwilling to show him how much it hurt that he'd start this with her only to leave. "That reminds me."

She reached over the side of the bed for his package, handed it to him. "Open this now. It's nothing. Just a fun thing."

He gave her a curious look, then pulled off the wrapping and opened the box, pulled out the small globe she'd bought him, hovering midair between two magnets repelling it with equal strength. "I bought this thinking I'd get you the world since I didn't know you'd be able to go so soon."

He smiled at the globe, gave it a spin, then lifted his head to include her in the smile. "Thank you. It's perfect, Krista."

One year. One year for her to fall even more deeply in love with him and then he'd be gone. "But I guess you'll be able to go for real now."

"I'll be taking an extended trip, yes." He spun the globe again, still smiling. "Which I sincerely hope will be my honeymoon."

Krista's mouth dropped. "Your honeymoon?"

"Would you like to come?"

"On your *honey*—" She stared at him, at his deep hazel eyes lit green in the candlelight. And instead of one year, she suddenly saw the rest of her life. "Are you asking me to marry you?"

"Not quite yet. But I will someday. Not too far off."

He put the globe down carefully, gathered her close and kissed her forehead and cheeks. "Since I found you in the dark, Krista, everything in my world has been brighter."

Tears. She didn't try to hide them this time. Another perfect fantasy—would he ever stop making them come true? "When that someday comes, I'll say yes. I love you, Seth."

"I love you, too." He nudged her nose tenderly with his. "And thank God you'll say yes. I was terrified you'd tell me to *get real*."

She laughed. "I don't think it gets realer than you and me."

"I agree." A soft chime came from downstairs and Seth grinned his sexy, already-familiar grin. "Midnight. Merry Christmas."

"Merry Christmas to you, too."

He frowned. "I didn't buy you a present. If you'd refused to come over, I couldn't stand having to look at whatever it was, knowing I'd never be able to give it to you. I'll make it up to you next year."

She waved him off. "Don't even think about it. In case you haven't noticed, I'm not much into the material side of life. Christmas is about love, remember?"

"I remember."

"And besides..." She kissed him, kissed him again and then was afraid she'd never be able to stop, eyes wide-open, looking into those of the man she loved. "All I want for Christmas is you."

Connect with...The HotWires!

A sizzling new three book miniseries
from popular author

Samantha Hunter

Start with Ian's story in
Fascination, on sale December 2005

Then get ready for Sarah's sexy tale in
Friction, on sale January 2006

And finish with E.J.'s finale in
Flirtation, on sale February 2006

The HotWires: this covert team sparks
desire...and danger.

Watch out!